No Way to Treat a Lady . . .

"Afternoon!" Pete said, doffing his new hat as he approached the woman. "Beautiful morning."

Amy barely nodded, giving the man little attention. She had learned long ago to discourage conversations with strange men, and although this one appeared presentable, there was just something about him that set her alarm bells ringing. She certainly didn't want to be rude, but she didn't want to talk to this stranger either.

"Yes, ma'am!" the man continued with a wide grin. "It is a very nice day. Are you new to Rock Springs?"

"I am," Amy said, turning away in an attempt to let him know she was not interested in a conversation.

But the moment she turned, Amy felt the tall stranger push hard up against her and then she heard the loud crack of a gunshot and felt a searing pain in her side. She cried out and pivoted while falling. The stranger fired a second shot, which Amy saw bite into the sidewalk and spit splinters.

The man started to yank his gun from its holster to finish her off, but suddenly and from what seemed like a great distance, she heard Custis shout.

One more shot and then Amy struck the boardwalk and lost consciousness . . .

TABOR EVANS

LONGARM

AND THE ROCK SPRINGS RECKONING

JOVE BOOKS, NEW YORK

BERKLEY PUBLISHING GROUP
Published by the Penguin Group
Penguin Group (USA) LLC
375 Hudson Street, New York, New York 10014

USA • Canada • UK • Ireland • Australia • New Zealand • India • South Africa • China

penguin.com

A Penguin Random House Company

LONGARM AND THE ROCK SPRINGS RECKONING

A Jove Book / published by arrangement with the author

For information, address: The Berkley Publishing Group,
a division of Penguin Group (USA) LLC,
375 Hudson Street, New York, New York 10014.

ISBN: 978-0-515-15488-7

PUBLISHING HISTORY
Jove mass-market edition / January 2015

PRINTED IN THE UNITED STATES OF AMERICA

10 9 8 7 6 5 4 3 2 1

Cover illustration by Milo Sinovcic.

Chapter 1

United States Deputy Marshal Custis Long was strolling along Cherry Creek after a day at the office, and it felt good to be outdoors enjoying the weather. It was mid-May and the air was cool, the trees had leafed out, and there wasn't a cloud in the deep blue Colorado sky. He was dressed in his usual brown tweed suit and vest, a blue-gray shirt with a shoestring tie, and a flat-brimmed hat that was dark brown in color. Being a handsome and tall man at six feet four inches, he always caught the attention of people . . . especially young women.

"Afternoon, ma'am," he said to each of the ladies he passed, many of whom blushed. And then to a well-dressed gentleman, "Afternoon, sir. Fine spring weather we're having, and it looks like our lakes are going to be full again this summer because there's so much snow up on the mountains."

"You can never have too much water," the older man agreed as he walked arm in arm with his portly, apple-cheeked wife. "Three years ago we hardly got any snow, and the town was worried about its water supply."

"Yes, it was," Longarm agreed, passing by.

The footpath along Cherry Creek was a popular place for people to stroll and admire the rippling stream and the cottonwoods flushed with their young, pale green leaves. Two boys about thirteen years old were fishing by the bridge and Longarm called, "Catch anything yet?"

One boy turned and shook his head. "They aren't favoring worms today, Marshal."

"Well, maybe you should try some cheese or marshmallows."

"All we got is the worms we dug out of the garden this morning."

"They bite best at sundown," Longarm called, checking his railroad pocket watch with the gold chain that was attached to a twin-barreled .44 caliber derringer. His Colt revolver bulged under his coat, and it rested butt-forward and was of the same caliber. Longarm was an expert shot, but he drew his pistol only in the most serious situations. Although he had killed a number of outlaws, murderers, thieves, and rapists in his law career, he was never eager to add to the growing list.

But suddenly, about a hundred yards upstream, he heard a woman's scream for help. Longarm drew his revolver and took off up the well-worn dirt path, running fast. The screams were coming from the heavy thickets, and Longarm burst into them ready to do battle with whoever was causing the woman such alarm.

"Help!" she yelled. "Somebody please help!"

Longarm fought his way through the heavy growth and came upon a young woman being attacked by two large and dirty men. The woman was on the ground with her dress pushed to her waist. One assailant was holding her arms pinned to the earth while the other was tearing off her underclothes.

"Stop!" Longarm shouted, taking aim at the men and cocking back the hammer of his pistol.

The pair froze and looked up at him. One said, "She's a whore, Marshal. She came here looking for business, and we're just about to give her some business. Ain't no need to draw that gun."

"Get away from her," Longarm ordered. "Do it now!"

The two men released the woman and stepped back. Longarm kept one eye on the attackers and his other on the woman, whose face was dirty and whose cheeks were wet with tears. "Are you all right, miss?"

"No, I'm not all right!" She climbed to her feet, pulled up her underpants, and tugged down her dress, which was covered with dirt and debris. "These bastards just tried to rape me. I want them arrested and thrown in jail!"

"I was just about to do that, but I wanted to make sure you were unharmed," Longarm said.

"But I *am* harmed! She held up her wrists to show Longarm the bruises. "These men were going to rape and then kill me!"

Longarm glanced at the pair. "What are your names?"

"Pete Rafter," the taller one said. "But she's lyin' to you, Marshal. We weren't going to rape her, and we sure as hell wouldn't have killed her."

"Not true, Pete!" the woman shrieked, her face contorted with rage. "You were both going to do me dirty!"

"Lucy, it'd be damned hard to do you dirty when you were *already* dirty," the second man scoffed.

"What's your name?" Longarm asked.

"Willie Benton."

"Where do you and your friend live?"

"In the woods, under the bridges, sometimes in stables. We don't have much money so we sleep wherever it's free."

"If you don't have any money, how were you going to pay Lucy for her services?"

The two attackers exchanged glances and both shrugged. Finally one said, "We was going to pay her a little something and owe her the rest."

"Owe me?" Lucy cried, wiping her cheeks dry and sneering at the pair. "You're both a pair of liars. I wouldn't give it to you if you paid me a *hundred* dollars each!"

"You didn't get a hundred dollars when someone broke your cherry when you was probably about ten years old," Pete snapped. "And now you don't get more'n two dollars a trick."

"I get five sometimes!" she shouted. "And I've gotten more."

Longarm dropped his gun to his side. He had seen this kind of thing too many times, and it had never set well with him. He was pretty sure that Lucy had agreed to come out and lie down in the bushes for these men for a few quick dollars. It was clear that she was a prostitute and of low morals. But what had happened was that when the two men had gotten her into the bushes and revealed that they had little or no money, Lucy had tried to leave and they'd not been willing to let her go before they had their pleasure.

"How much money do you men have altogether?" Longarm asked.

"I got two dollars," Pete confessed. "And a good pocket knife."

"And you?" Longarm asked, turning to the other.

"A dollar and change."

Longarm didn't believe them. "Both of you pull all your pockets out and empty them."

"Marshal . . ." Pete whined.

"Do it or I'm taking you to jail."

"Jail ain't so bad if they feed you and the bunks aren't alive with fleas and ticks," Willie pointed out.

"Empty your pockets, and give everything to me."

They both emptied their pockets and handed their money and possessions to Longarm, who said, "Looks to be about five dollars here with all the change, and that is a good knife."

"It was given to me by my father," Pete said. "I place considerable sentimental value on that knife."

"Well," Longarm mused. "This knife would bring about three dollars in a pawn shop or in a saloon." He turned to Lucy. "I can throw them in jail, but then you'd get nothing. Or," he added, "I can give you the knife and their money and we all just walk away."

"They go free?" Lucy snorted in outrage and anger.

"Not free," Longarm corrected. "If you sell the knife and add that to all their money, you're going to make seven or eight dollars, and you didn't have to let them inside of you."

"I got bruises!"

"Then I'll take them to jail and they'll get a few weeks of free food and a roof over their heads."

"We'd be willing to do that," Willie said. "But no prison."

"No prison," Longarm agreed.

"I don't want to give her my father's good knife, dammit!"

"It isn't up to you, Pete. What'll it be, Lucy? Seven dollars, or they go to jail and you get nothing?"

"I'll take the money and his damned knife," she declared, "but only 'cause I can see that it means something to him."

"I loved my pa," Pete said bitterly. "It's the only thing that I got left from him."

"He was probably as big an asshole as you turned out to be," Lucy snapped, taking the knife and the money.

Longarm hadn't wanted to take Pete and Willie to jail because he knew it was already overflowing with men just like this disreputable pair and the local sheriff was on a tight budget.

"We have a deal," he said to the pair as he holstered his gun. "But I'll tell you something . . . if I ever hear of you boys attacking a woman again . . . even a whore . . . I'll see that you go to prison for *years*. Understood?"

They nodded.

"And I don't want to see either one of you hanging around Cherry Creek looking for someone to roll for their money or begging. Is that also understood?"

Again, they nodded.

"Then get out of here! I understand that there is work up in the mountains to be had and you men are young and strong enough to handle a pick and a shovel."

"I got a bad back," Pete whined.

"I ain't no damned miner or stable hand," Willie growled.

"Well," Longarm told them, "you boys had better find honest work or you'll surely end up in prison or worse. Now get out of here."

Pete shot a nasty look at Lucy. "You weren't worth that knife . . . not if I traded it for ten pokes between your skinny legs!"

"You bastard!" she yelled, balling her fists and coming at him.

Longarm blocked her path and said, "It's still a nice day, Lucy. Why don't we go for a little walk so you can cool down and then I'll take you out for dinner."

The anger washed out of her face. She brushed at the dirt and debris in her long black hair. "You'd do that with me . . . in public?"

"Sure would."

Lucy took a deep breath. "All right, Marshal. I'd be proud to accompany you to a nice meal . . . and I do prefer my steak cooked on the rare side. And apple pie . . . fresh, you know."

"I know just the place," he said, offering her his arm.

Lucy took his arm, shot a hateful glance at Pete and Willie, and then she lifted her dress, swung her narrow butt around, and farted loudly. "That's what I give you for seven dollars, you assholes!"

"Bitch!" Pete spat.

"Wormy whore," Willie hissed.

Longarm felt Lucy try to pull away and attack the pair but he held her steady. "Let it go," he whispered. "You came out ahead and now we're going to have a nice, pleasant dinner together."

To the two men, he said, "Get out of my sight!" Immediately, they ran down the path and disappeared from view.

Lucy turned to Longarm and asked, "You married, Marshal?"

"Nope."

"Sweet on some special woman?"

"I like most all women."

"Even me?"

"Yes, even you," Longarm said, trying not to smile. "You may be a whore, but you've got spunk and I think you might have some hopes for the future."

"Not me," she told him. "I'm going to die of the French disease or by the gun or the knife."

"You can change your life."

"How?" she asked, looking up at him.

"Maybe," Longarm said, "we can talk about just that over a couple of rare steaks and slices of apple pie."

Lucy giggled. "You can do the talking 'cause you're the one who's buyin'!" She bumped him hard with her hip. "And who knows what will happen later?"

"Nothing will happen."

"I ain't got the French disease yet, Marshal. I swear to you I would never give it to someone as kind as yourself."

Longarm laughed outright as they passed the boys fishing along the creek. He saw that one had just pulled a fish from the water and it was decent eating size.

"They must have liked those worms of yours after all!"

"Yep," the boy said, staring at Lucy with a grimace. "Where'd you find *her*?"

"Never you mind," Longarm told them as he and Lucy headed into town.

"Those seem like a couple of nice boys," Lucy offered. "I had a brother that looked like the taller one. And he liked to fish all the time."

"What was his name?"

"Horace."

"Horace what?"

"Horace Potter."

"So you're Lucy Potter."

"Yes, I am."

"Well, I'm Custis Long and I'd prefer you just call me Custis rather than Marshal."

"I'll do 'er," Lucy promised. "And since you're bein' so nice to me, you can call me whatever damn thing you want."

"I'll call you Lucy."

"Good enough. Where do you live, Custis?"

"Oh, I have an apartment not far from here."

"Maybe I'd like to see it after we eat."

"Don't you have one of your own?"

She rolled her eyes. "I sleep with the other girls at Maggie's Place. But I don't have no one telling me when I have to be there. Maggie just lets us come and go, as long as we stay sober and don't smoke opium or try and rob the customers."

"How long have you worked at Maggie's Place?"

"Two years."

"That's a lot of men."

"I know," she said. "Long ago I lost count."

"Any of them ever hurt you?"

"Of course. It's part of the job."

"You need to find a different kind of a job, Lucy."

Her laugh was hard and cold. "Sure, maybe I could go to your office tomorrow and they'd hire me as a United States marshal and I'd wear a shiny badge and make good money. What do you think?"

"I think you've got a cynical streak as wide as your shoulders and as deep as your heart."

She paused in mid-step. "The thing of it is, Custis, I don't really have a heart anymore. Can't afford one. When I had a heart, it always got broken. Better for a whore like me to have no heart at all."

"Let's not talk like this anymore," he said. "Have you ever eaten at Abner's Steak House?"

"Of course not, but I've walked by it a thousand times. Nice, respectable men and women go into Abner's Steak House. Whores like me don't even dream of entering such fine places."

Longarm studied her out of the corner of his eye. "Let's go into that dress shop just up the street and find you a clean, pretty one. You'll shine up a lot with a new dress."

Lucy stopped dead in her tracks, and then she covered her face and began to cry.

Oh Lord, Longarm thought, *Lucy still does have a heart.*

Chapter 2

Longarm knew the woman who owned the dress shop . . . in fact, he knew her very, very well. Her name was Sarah Freeman, and she was in her early thirties and quite attractive. She had pinned her hopes last year on snagging him as a prized husband, but when Longarm had told her in no uncertain terms that he intended to remain a bachelor and a deputy marshal, Sarah moved on to other and better prospects. As far as he knew now, she was still unmarried and on the prowl. Her sights were set very high, and Longarm doubted she would ever find a man that met her impossibly high standards for a husband.

"Hello, Sarah," he said, pushing Lucy into the dress shop.

She was standing behind the counter, messing with a pencil and paper, but when she heard his familiar voice, she looked up with a happy smile, which quickly faded when her eyes came to rest on Lucy.

"Custis, what a pleasant surprise."

"I agree," he said, trying not to think about how long and lovely her bare legs were. "This is Miss Lucy Potter."

Sarah stared at the dirty whore and said, "How nice to meet you, Lucy," in a way that made it clear she was not at all pleased to have Lucy in her high-toned dress shop. "What can I do for you today?"

"Lucy needs a new dress."

"So I can tell. But I'm afraid that I just don't have anything that would . . . would do for her."

"Oh, surely you must have something," Longarm persisted. He marched over to a rack of dresses and took one off the hook, holding it up and saying, "This looks like it would fit her."

"It *won't* fit," Sarah insisted.

"I think it will," Longarm said, going over to Lucy, who hadn't said a word yet. "Here, hold this up against you and let me take a look."

Lucy's eyes were downcast. She took the dress without hardly looking at it and pressed it to her body.

"Do you like it?" Longarm asked.

"It's okay, I guess."

"I think it looks great on you," Longarm said, trying to keep his tone light and cheery. "How much is the dress?"

"Twelve dollars, but—"

"We'll take it."

Sarah said nothing but just glared at Longarm. The silence grew icy and uncomfortable and so he reached for his wallet, found the money, and paid for the dress by slamming the bills down on Sarah's paperwork.

"I don't suppose you have a—"

"No I don't!" Sarah hissed. "Now I'd like you both to leave."

"We were just on our way out your door," Longarm snapped, snatching up the dress. "Ready, Lucy?"

"I *am* ready to leave this uppity bitch," Lucy said, finally looking at the storekeeper. "Have a nice evening, ma'am, just like me and Custis are planning to do."

"I'm sure that I don't care what kind of an evening you intend to have," Sarah managed to choke out. "Custis, shame on you!"

He smiled and tipped his hat before he wordlessly took Lucy's arm and headed out the door, not bothering to close it in his wake.

"I should wash up and brush my hair," Lucy finally said as they walked along the boardwalk. "Too pretty a dress to wear when I'm so dirty."

Longarm could not deny her logic. "I know where you can take a quick bath and clean up."

"Where?"

"My apartment will do."

Lucy looked up at him with a big, happy smile. "Now you're talkin'," she said.

"But just to clean up," he added quickly. "Nothing more."

"Sure," she told him with that happy smile still plastered on her face. It was a face that showed some years of hard living, but it was a pretty face, or at least Longarm thought it might be when it was washed. And that black hair was dull and tangled but it was long and thick . . . it would look nice after it was washed and brushed.

Lucy, he decided, was a diamond in the rough. *Maybe she really can turn her life around with a little help, direction, and encouragement,* he thought.

"Nice apartment," Lucy said, pirouetting around and taking everything in. "You lived here long?"

"About a year."

She studied the furniture and then walked into his small but efficient kitchen. "Got an ice box and everything, huh?"

"Yeah, the iceman comes by twice a week."

Lucy opened some cabinets. "See that you don't eat much here."

"I usually eat out," Longarm said.

"Handsome rugs and I especially like that bed of yours. Nice and big." Before Longarm could stop her, Lucy ran into his bedroom and flopped down on the bed. "Pretty soft, too!"

"Look," Longarm said as sternly as he could, "this is my place and I don't want you to get to thinking that it could be your place."

"Of course not!" She grinned. "I already told you that I have a room at Maggie's Place."

"Well, fine," he said gruffly, already beginning to think he had made a big mistake by bringing her to his apartment. "I'm going down the hall to draw you a hot bath. It won't take long and I suggest you might start combing your hair while we wait on the hot water."

"You got brushes?"

"In the bathroom."

"My underclothes aren't too clean either," Lucy commented as he was leaving. "Maybe I should just wear them in the bathtub and scrub 'em up while you scrub my back and wash my hair."

Longarm froze in mid-stride. "I don't intend to scrub your back or wash your hair."

"It'd be a big favor if you did, though. I haven't had a man take care of me even a little in longer than I can recall. It sure would be a pleasure."

Longarm headed down the hall and found the bathtub

room. It was used by everyone on his floor, who were all bachelors like himself. Sometimes a man could be hired to bring up some extra hot water, but mostly the baths were at best lukewarm. He checked to make sure that no one was using the room, then he turned on the water and started filling the tub. Having running water was one of the main reasons he had rented this apartment on the ground floor.

What have I done now? he wondered as the tub slowly filled. He had not wanted to say anything, but not only was Lucy dirty . . . she smelled terrible. The idea of putting her in a nice, clean dress and then taking a stinky woman to Abner's Steak House just didn't sit right with him, and if other patrons were as repelled by her smell as he was, it would become an issue. Better, much better to get her scrubbed up and clean first.

"Is it ready for me?" Lucy yelled from his apartment door.

"Yeah, bring a towel and a bar of soap and come on down."

"Where are your towels and soap?"

"In my hall closet on the right."

Longarm was turning off the water when he heard a wolf whistle, and when he twisted around toward the hallway, there was Lucy just as naked as the day she was born but a lot more shapely.

"Damn," a man said, standing in the doorway. "Where did you come from, honey?"

"Maggie's Place! Stop by and see me sometime."

"How about we skip Maggie's and you come on into my room right now!"

"No thanks. I'm with Marshal Custis Long, I'll have you know."

"Lucy!" Longarm shouted. "You . . . aww, the hell with it."

Lucy had a *very* nice figure. Big breasted and her legs were long and shapely. The only detraction were the many bruises he saw on her body, and he wondered if they were caused by Pete and Willie or by earlier customers.

"You shouldn't have just walked naked down the entire hallway," Longarm complained. "That fella is going to tell everyone in the building what he saw."

"Good, maybe they'll all come looking for me at Maggie's Place and I'll make a lot of money."

Lucy laughed but Longarm didn't think it was a bit funny. "Climb in," he ordered, closing the door.

"What do you think?" Lucy asked, stepping into the bathtub and cupping her hands under her breasts then turning around slowly so he could see her at every delicious angle. "Not bad, huh? I still got my shape."

"Yes, you do have that." Longarm picked up the bar of soap, dipped it into the tub, and began to soap up her long black hair. "How long has it been since you bathed, Lucy?"

"I get a bath every three or four days. Maggie charges fifty cents and I don't like to spend the money but some of the men who pound on me are as rough and smelly as old dogs. Ohhh, that feels nice . . . don't stop."

Longarm had no intention of stopping. He soaped her hair thoroughly, and then despite his earlier words, he scrubbed her back while she sighed and moaned with pleasure. "You're pretty good at this," she told him. "I'll bet you've had practice with tons of women."

"Some."

"Well," she said, grinning. "Now you can soap up my tits, and I'll bet if we tried, we could both get into this tub and jiggle around a little or whatever."

"Never mind." He handed her a washcloth that someone had left on a hook and the soap. "Wash yourself up good then I'll drain the tub, which looks like it is about half mud, and we'll get some clean water to rinse your hair and body off."

"I got nice hair, don't I. Everyone loves my hair and my legs and my nice titties. Don't you?"

"You have beautiful hair," he said in spite of himself. "And the other things you mentioned are nice, too. How long have you been a whore?"

"Oh," she said, leaning her head back against the rim of the tub and staring up at the ceiling. "I had my first boy when I was twelve and then I had my first man about six months later . . . it was my Uncle Jim. He said that I shouldn't sleep with boys because they didn't know how to pleasure a girl and their clumsiness could cause pain. Uncle Jim showed me how a man should fornicate with a woman and how to make her feel real nice."

"How old was Jim?"

"Oh, I don't know. He wasn't so old that he couldn't do it three times a day and still want for more. He was always after me when my pa wasn't around. I finally ran away when I was fifteen because nothing he ever did to me felt real nice."

"What about your mother?"

"She died when I was ten. A rattlesnake bit her when she was chopping wood on our little farm back near Fort Smith, Arkansas. It was real sad."

"Do you have any brothers or sisters besides Horace?"

"A sister I haven't seen or heard from in years. But I heard Horace has done well up in Rock Springs, Wyoming. He owns a big ranch and a bank in town. Can you imagine a brother of mine being a rich banker?"

Longarm had to smile. "Actually, Lucy, I can well imagine your brother being a banker and you being a successful person."

"I am *already* successful. Not a girl at Maggie's Place gets asked for more than me, and I make more money than any girl there. So what do you have to say about that?"

"I'd say that, if you went out to Cherry Creek to get laid by the likes of Pete and Willie, that's not being real successful."

Lucy was quiet for a few moments while she slowly rubbed the bar of nice-smelling soap around her breasts . . . first one and then the other. "Custis, to be honest, I know I'm walking down death's road doin' what I do. Yet I never could turn down a man wanting to pay me for what I mostly enjoy so it just seems to me there's mutual satisfaction taken on both sides . . . only I get paid."

"In ten years . . . if you're even still alive . . . you'll look old and feel older," Longarm warned. "I know you've seen the girls that have gotten older at Maggie's Place and how sad and pathetic their lives become when they're no longer the prettiest or youngest whores in the room."

"Yeah," Lucy said after few moments, "I can see that happening to me. But I been promised so much by men and never once did they do the good things they said they wanted to do for me. Why, I'll bet if one man has been humping me and asked for my hand in marriage, there are a hundred who have done the same. Mostly they were drunk and none of 'em meant a word spoken out of their lyin' lips."

"Do you want to change your life?"

She looked up at him. "There's an old sayin', Custis, and it is that you can't make a silk purse out of a sow's ear. And that's the truth."

"How old are you?"

"Twenty-five."

"You can still do it."

"Are you a preacher or something? I mean, are you one of those holier-than-thou folks trying to save my wicked soul?"

"No, I'm trying to save your wicked *life*."

She laughed. "Well, I surely do appreciate the sentiment. And I am grateful. Real grateful. Pull your pants down and I'll show you how grateful I am right now and right here while I sit in this bathtub."

Longarm shook his head. "Just . . . just finish up and let's get you rinsed off and dried."

"What about my dirty underwear?"

"Wear 'em or not, that's your decision."

"I won't wear them now that I'm so clean. But what about you?"

"What about me?" Longarm asked.

"There will be a lot of bad talk after you're seen with me."

"That's true," he admitted. "And I may never hear the end of it."

She reached out and squeezed his hand with all her might. "Custis, I don't want to shame you in front of people you know. So if . . . if you don't want to take me out to that nice place, I'll understand. I really will."

Something inside Longarm softened, and he said, "Aw hell, Lucy, with your new dress on and your tits jiggling under that thin material, you will be the center of attention and admiration. So we're going and I'll be proud to take your arm and sit with you at the best table, where everyone who comes in will see us together and most men will be down-right envious."

Lucy swallowed hard. "You're a really *good* man, Custis. Best one I've been with in the longest time."

"Well," he said, feeling a little embarrassed, "let's get you dried off and that hair combed and then we'll go off and have us a fine steak, a few whiskeys, and a high old time all the way around."

"I can't wait!"

Actually, Longarm realized, he was pretty excited about taking Lucy out for a steak and some drinks. And while the word about him taking one of Maggie's whores out to a nice establishment would quickly spread across downtown Denver, he didn't really give a damn. Sure, women like Sarah Freeman and her type would turn their noses up now whenever he passed. However, Denver was a big city and there were a lot of other lovely and lonely women who wouldn't ever care who he escorted to dinner as long as he gave them his loving and undivided attention.

Chapter 3

"Well," Lucy said as they stood outside Maggie's Place, "I sure do thank you for everything."

"Our steaks were just right," Longarm said. "And you looked lovely."

Lucy's eyes glistened. "I don't even think most people inside even realized who I am and what I do for money."

"I'm sure that they didn't," Longarm agreed.

"You know I left my dirty underwear at your apartment."

"So you did."

"Can I come around soon and pick them up?"

"Of course. Tomorrow evening would be fine. How about around six o'clock? We can even go out to eat someplace although it won't be as nice or expensive as Abner's Steak House."

"I'd love that!" Lucy gushed. She reached up on her tiptoes and gave him a kiss full on the lips.

Longarm grinned until he glanced aside and saw two

men going into Maggie's Place. One of them shouted, "Hey, Lucy, come on! You're the one I want again tonight!"

"Be right there," she said, her shoulders slumping.

Longarm felt awful. He wanted to help this girl, but he didn't know how that might work and the last thing he needed was to take care of someone. He traveled a lot on assignments, and when he was home, he often preferred just to enjoy some solitude. Still, he had a feeling that Lucy was, at heart, a very fine person who had started off by being raped and then used and had just never really had a chance to be a respectable, happy woman.

Lucy Potter deserves a chance to have a long, happy life, he said to himself as he walked away.

At the corner, he turned back just in time to see Lucy and the two men climbing up the porch steps and entering the whorehouse. The sight of it took away all the enjoyment and satisfaction he'd felt while treating her to a really special dinner.

Longarm was rather distracted all the next day at the office. He had never liked riding a desk, but there were the obligatory forms and paperwork to fill out and he doggedly worked away at a stack. In midafternoon, he got up and went in to chat with his friend and boss, Marshal Billy Vail. Billy had long since been promoted out of the field, and now he seemed to be content with a bigger paycheck and an office and supervisory job. Billy had put on quite a lot of weight since his days of being a deputy marshal, but he still had a keen interest in what was going on out in the field, and while he supervised six deputies, Longarm was his clear favorite and most trusted law officer.

"How's it going, Billy?" Longarm asked, closing the door

behind him and not waiting to be invited to sit down in one of Billy's plush office chairs.

"Oh, about the same as usual. We've got some problems back in Washington, and sometimes that rubs off on us out here in the field offices. But there's nothing that I can't handle." Billy leaned back in his chair and linked his fingers behind his head. He was of average height and still quite handsome. One of the things Longarm liked the best about his boss and friend was that Billy's demeanor almost never changed. He didn't get rattled or angry unless someone in his office really screwed up badly . . . which could happen. The man was happily married to a good woman, and his kids were respectful and doing well in school. Billy owned a nice little house, and he was looking forward to a pension at the end of his career and maybe even a move to a warmer winter climate.

"You got any assignments coming my way?" Longarm asked. "I've been desk bound for over a week and you know how much I hate that."

"Yeah, I know. Even I detest being cooped up indoors when the weather is turning so nice. Me and the missus planted a garden this past weekend, although we might be jumping the gun because it can still freeze this time of the year. But you know how much we enjoy our homegrown tomatoes, string beans, corn, and cucumbers."

"I sure do," Longarm said. "And I always appreciate it when you bring some of that harvest down to the office so us poor bachelors can have fresh produce."

"Maybe," Billy mused, "you ought to think about buying a house so you could have a garden."

Longarm scoffed. "And who would tend it when I'm out of town trying to catch the criminals?"

"Well . . . well, you'd probably be able to find a reliable boy or girl in the neighborhood to take care of things in your absence."

"That's okay," Longarm said. "I like my apartment and I'm not ready to start a garden or worry about the upkeep of a house."

"Houses in Denver tend to be good investments, and you have to start thinking about the day when you no longer want to be riding the outlaw's back trail."

"I'll give it some thought," Longarm promised, knowing he wouldn't.

"No you won't," Billy said with a short, good-natured laugh. "I quit working out in the field when I turned forty and you're still a long ways shy of being that old. Custis, you have to remember that time does have a way of sneaking up on a man . . . even one like you."

"Can we change the subject?"

"Sure."

"So when can I go on another assignment?"

"Maybe next week something will turn up."

"I hope so because I'm going stir crazy at my desk looking at forms and wanted posters. But there is something else I would like to talk to you about."

"Shoot."

"I helped a young woman down by Cherry Creek who was being attacked by two unsavory men."

Billy's smile evaporated. "Why didn't you tell me that the first thing this morning? Did you kill or wound them?"

"No."

"Then you must have arrested them and taken them to jail."

"I didn't do that either," Longarm said. "They claimed that

the woman was a whore who works and stays at Maggie's Place . . . and it turned out that was the truth. They said that she'd come with them on her own accord and they'd agreed to pay her for a romp in the bushes down near the creek."

"That's not a good idea," Billy said. "A lot of nice families and people stroll along there when the weather turns nice, and the last thing they want to see is some whore servicing a couple of guys."

"I know," Longarm said. "But this . . . this whore . . . well, she was bruised, and I had the feeling that she was being raped."

"That's a strong word to call it when a woman from Maggie's goes down to the river to do the nasty with a couple of men for money."

"True," Longarm agreed. "But they were roughing her up, and she was yelling for help so I came to her aid."

"Of course you did," Billy said. "You're a good lawman and a gentleman despite your reputation as an unrepentant womanizer. So what is this about? They got rough, you came to her aid, and then since you didn't draw your gun or blood or even take them to jail . . . it must have worked out fine."

"Well, yes and no. The woman's name is Lucy Potter, and she was kind of shook up and dirtied up so I took her to my apartment and helped her out."

Billy began to shake his head. "Don't tell me . . . you screwed her and found out she had the French disease."

"No, I didn't do anything of the sort," Longarm shot back, vexed by the fact that his boss was making unsavory assumptions. "I bought her a new dress and she bathed at my place and I took her out for a really nice steak dinner at Abner's Steak House. We drank some wine and ate and talked a long time and—"

"Then you took her back to your apartment and screwed her."

"No, dammit!"

"Well, what *did* you do with her?"

"I took her back to Maggie's and said good-bye."

Billy scowled and leaned forward, elbows on his desk. "So why are you telling me all of this?"

"Good question," Longarm said. "You see, Lucy was raped by her old Uncle Jim when she was twelve and she's been used hard ever since. The girl, as near as I can tell, has never had a fair chance at making an honest and respectable living."

Billy scoffed. "Don't all whores tell you they were raped young and they just never had a break in their entire life? Custis, don't tell me that you've fallen for the oldest line in the book!"

"I'd like to help her," Longarm snapped. "And if you can't give me some advice on that subject, then we're through with this conversation."

Longarm started to get out of this chair and stomp back to his desk but Billy said, "Wait a minute! Don't go off mad at me."

"Well, why shouldn't I be mad? I wanted some advice and all you can do is tell me that Lucy is a liar and a manipulator and that I'm a fool for helping her or believing a word she told me. Isn't that right?"

"Look, Custis, maybe I'm being too harsh in my judgment. Perhaps there are a few decent whores who could . . . with help . . . go straight and live long, happy lives. It's just that I've never heard of one."

"Well, Lucy might be the first."

"Okay," Billy said, holding his hands up. "How are you going to do it?"

"I have no idea."

"Surely you are not going to invite the woman to live in your apartment."

Longarm shrugged. "The idea has crossed my mind."

"Well, then cross it right out of your mind, Custis! The first time you go off on an assignment, she'll invite some of her favored customers into your place to try your bed . . . then they'll steal everything that isn't nailed to the floor."

"You're saying it would be a disaster."

"Hell yes, that's what I'm saying! Custis, just drop this entire, foolish idea you have of saving Lucy Potter's soiled soul. Never think of or see her again."

"She's coming by at six o'clock for her dirty underwear."

Billy dropped his face into his hands and groaned. "I don't think I want to hear anything more about this."

Longarm stood up. "And I don't think I want to tell you any more about Miss Lucy Potter."

"Good."

Longarm headed for the door.

"Leave her dirty underwear in the hallway and lock your door, Custis. That's what any man with a lick of good sense would do!"

Longarm slammed his boss's door hard and stomped over to his desk. He was damned mad and disappointed in his friend. However, the truth of the matter was that Billy was probably more right than wrong about what he should do at six o'clock this evening when Lucy came around.

Chapter 4

"Hello, Custis, darling," she said when he opened his apartment door. "Have you missed me?"

Longarm started to say something and then froze. Lucy had two black eyes, a swollen lip, and fresh bloodstains across the front of her new dress.

"Lucy, what in blazes happened?"

"I had trouble with Pete and Willie. Pete wanted his father's knife back, and I wouldn't give it to him so he and Willie got rough."

"When and where did this happen?"

"This afternoon. He and Willie came by and demanded to see me, but Maggie wouldn't let them inside. She told them to go away and leave me alone. But when I went out to get something later that day, they were waiting for me. When I told Pete to leave me alone and that I didn't have his father's knife on me, he pulled me off the sidewalk where we couldn't be seen and both he and Willie began hitting me over and over in the face and the stomach."

Lucy suddenly cried out and clutched her midsection. Her eyes rolled up in her head, and she moaned just before she began to fall. Longarm carried her to his bed. "How bad is the pain?"

"It's terrible," she whispered. "I . . . I coughed up a lot of blood on my way over and I don't feel good at all."

"I'm going for a doctor," Longarm said without hesitation. "Just lie here nice and easy and I'll be right back!"

"No!" she begged. "Just . . . just stay with me. The pain comes but it also goes. I just need a little rest and I'll be fine."

"We'll let the doctor decide that."

Longarm knew Doc Hamilton well. The man was very dedicated to his profession and not just some quack who had never gone to medical school. "I won't be gone more than twenty minutes," he promised. "And I'll lock the door behind me so that you'll be safe. Just lie still and try to relax."

"Could I have a drink of water before you go . . . or better yet, some whiskey?"

"I don't think whiskey is what you need," Longarm told her as he rushed to get the water. When he returned, he had to hold Lucy's head up from his pillow and she had trouble swallowing. Her skin was ice-cold. "Just lie easy and I'll be right back."

Lucy tried to grab his sleeve to stop him, but Longarm was already racing out the door. He ran down two blocks to Dr. Albert Hamilton's office. "I have a friend that needs to see the doctor right now," he said to the man's wife. "Where is the doc?"

Mrs. Hamilton was in her fifties, a nice, plump woman who was always in control no matter what kind of emergency took place. "I'm afraid that Albert is out on a call. Custis, you really look extremely upset. Did you shoot someone again?"

"There's a woman in my apartment who was attacked earlier today and is in serious pain. She said she's coughed up blood."

"Oh dear," Mrs. Hamilton said, "that *does* sound serious. But Albert might be gone for hours on his call."

"Is there another doctor you can recommend?"

"Not at this time of the evening."

Longarm paced back and forth for a few moments then stopped. "Can *you* help?"

"Perhaps. We can leave a note for Albert telling him about this emergency situation. While I'm getting some medicines together, write your address down on a slip of paper and a sentence or two about the patient."

"Mrs. Hamilton, we really need to hurry," Longarm said, trying to keep the rising panic out of his voice. "Lucy is in serious trouble."

"What happened?"

"She was attacked and beaten by two rough men. They punched her in the face and the stomach."

"I'll bring bandages and salves for her face. But it's the stomach pain that we have to worry about and I'm not really qualified to help with an internal injury."

"And you don't even know where your husband is right now?"

"I know where he is, but he can't leave his patient. She's having her baby, but without my husband at her side, she may die . . . she may die anyway. Albert looked very grim and upset when he left here a few hours ago."

"I understand." Longarm grabbed a sheet of paper from the desk, found a pencil, and wrote down his name, address, and a short note of explanation. "Are you sure he'll see this note?"

"Yes," the woman called from another room. "My husband always looks at the desk to see if there are any emergency messages."

Minutes later, Longarm was escorting the woman down the street as quickly as she could move. "I hope she'll be all right," he said.

"We'll certainly pray hard for her," Mrs. Hamilton said breathlessly. "And perhaps my husband will return shortly, see our message, and come right over. Please, Marshal, could you slow down just a little bit? My heart can't take this kind of strain, and we don't want the doctor to have *two* women to treat in addition to the one in labor."

"Sorry," he apologized, slowing down. Longarm felt ashamed of himself for not considering that Mrs. Hamilton was a large and certainly not a young woman. If her heart failed while she was trying to keep up with him, Longarm knew he would never forgive himself. The sun had gone down and it was chilly; the lack of sunlight turned his mood even darker.

It seemed to take an hour to get back to his apartment with Mrs. Hamilton in tow, but in fact, it was probably less than fifteen minutes. And even though Longarm had drastically slowed the pace, the heavy older woman was still breathless and struggling. He even had to help her up the two steps to get to the front door of his building.

When he unlocked his door and they hurried inside, Longarm ran across his living room into the bedroom. Lucy was lying just as he'd left her but now there was blood on the sheets and bed covers and she was barely breathing.

"Oh dear!" Mrs. Hamilton cried, rushing to the bedside, throwing back the covers, and then quickly unbuttoning Lucy's dress.

When she did that, both she and Longarm gasped in shock because Lucy's chest, ribs, and stomach were a mass of bruises.

"She has been beaten savagely!" Mrs. Hamilton said in a hushed, shocked voice as she took Lucy's pulse and then placed her ear close to Lucy's mouth to gauge her breathing.

"Is she going to die?"

"I don't know, but it doesn't look good."

"Anything you can do?"

"Besides prayer, I have some lotion to put under her nose that will help her breathe a little easier."

"What about medicine?"

"The poor woman is unconscious. She couldn't get any medicine down. It's clear even to me that she has some serious internal injuries to her organs."

"There must be *something* more we can do!"

The doctor's wife tried to smile. "Is she your lady friend, and does she have any next of kin we should contact?"

"She is my friend and has a wealthy brother up in Rock Springs, Wyoming, named Horace Potter."

"But you don't know how to contact this man?"

"No."

Mrs. Hamilton started to say something but then seemed to change her mind. "Well, we'll just have to wait and see."

"I'm not good at waiting."

"Then you should try and exercise patience. And as for this poor young woman, it seems to me that she is too thin and she has not been well taken care of. I see old bruises and signs of abuse."

"It's a long, sad story."

"Yes, I imagine it is. Have you known her long?"

"No."

"Does she work?"

"Mrs. Hamilton, I'd rather not talk right now. I know who did this to her, and I mean to find and arrest them."

"They must be *terrible* brutes!"

"They are," Longarm agreed, trying to harness and control the anger building deep inside.

"It is so very evil to do such a cruel thing."

Longarm managed to nod his head. He turned away with his fists knotted. His face was grim and he had a terrible urge to head out into the night and hunt down Pete and Willie and beat them both to death.

Suddenly, Lucy's eyes shot open and her head rolled back and forth on her pillow. Her lips moved and they could hear rasping whispers from deep in her throat. Mrs. Hamilton bent over to hear her better.

"What's she saying?" Longarm asked, straining to listen.

The lips stopped moving, Lucy's head stopped rolling frantically back and forth on her pillow, and a last breath sighed from her lungs.

Longarm had seen many men die . . . not so many women . . . but he knew Lucy Potter was gone.

"Mrs. Hamilton, what did she whisper with her last breath?"

"She said she loved you and that you should tell her brother she was sorry for being a shameful whore and an embarrassment to him."

Longarm whirled and left the room. He was filled with so much rage and pain that he dared not even try to speak.

When he found Willie Benton and Pete Rafter, he would consider himself no longer bound by laws and his badge would not be on his person. He would kill Pete and Willie while exacting a savage revenge.

Chapter 5

Longarm paid for Lucy Potter's proper funeral . . . a nice casket and lots of flowers. He knew a preacher who didn't preach damnation and told the man that while Lucy had been a prostitute, she had possessed a loving heart and that all-important fact should be emphasized in the eulogy. Longarm even placed an ad in the *Denver News* although he doubted anyone would care about Lucy's funeral or bother to attend.

He was wrong. On the breezy but sunny day of the funeral, Madam Maggie Maguire showed up with five of her girls all dressed finely in black lace and satin. In addition, none other than the dress shop owner, Miss Sarah Freeman, came wearing a stylish black dress, hat, and veil.

The sermon was short but powerful, and there wasn't a dry eye among the mourners. Longarm had only known Lucy for less than twenty-four hours, but she'd left him with a sharp and unexpected hollow feeling inside. When the grave was covered and the flowers were laid across the mound,

Longarm spoke for a moment with the undertaker and handed him another twenty dollars for a fine marble headstone.

"Usually," the undertaker whispered, "we have the date of birth along with the date of death."

"It's not important," Longarm replied, "but if you must have a date, have this her twenty-sixth birthday."

"That seems rather young, don't you think? I would have guessed her to be more like thirty-six."

"All right. Thirty-six," Longarm snapped. "But she might not have been that old because she had a very hard unfair life."

"I understand. And where was Miss Potter born?" the man asked solicitously.

"Fort Smith, Arkansas."

"Should I send my condolences to her family?"

"No. She has a brother named Horace Potter, who is living in Rock Springs, Wyoming. I travel through there on the train often, and the next time I do, I'll try to look the man up and tell him about Lucy's passing. But she wasn't close to him and I suspect he didn't want anyone associating him with a sister who had turned to prostitution."

"Understandable, but still regrettable," the undertaker said. "Also I was wondering—"

"Excuse me, Marshal. Could we have a word in private?" Maggie Maguire was in her forties, still handsome, and it was rumored that she was very well-to-do. She was tall and her eyes were as hard as obsidian, but now they were filled with tears.

"Of course," Longarm said, offering the woman his arm and then leading her off so that they could speak confidentially. "And I want to say that I think it is very good of you and your girls to come to Lucy's funeral."

"Good?" Maggie said, shrugging her shoulders sadly. "Why, we *all* loved Lucy. She was a jewel among rubble stone, and we treasured the time we had with her. I am extremely upset about what happened, and I want to know if her killers are being brought to justice."

"I know their names and their faces," Longarm said. "And I have been looking for Pete Rafter and Willie Benton, but they seem to have disappeared. Given that they know I was fond of Miss Potter and a United States marshal, it would not surprise me in the least if they have quickly left Denver for parts unknown."

"I see," Maggie said, eyebrows knitting almost together. "And how will they be found and brought to trial for the murder of my favorite girl?"

"I've made it a personal mission to track them down to the ends of the earth if necessary. Rest assured, Miss Maguire, I will not let them go free and I will bring them to a hard and well-deserved justice."

Maggie Maguire's face twisted with hatred, and she reached into her purse and pulled out a sealed envelope.

"What's this?"

"It's a thousand dollars."

"I don't want your money, Miss Maguire."

"It's not mine alone," she said. "Some of it was earned by my girls . . . they all loved Lucy and they want her killers brought to rope or bullet justice. I am hoping and counting on you, Marshal Long, to see that our wishes are fulfilled."

Longarm slipped the envelope into his inside coat pocket. "I'll take your money," he decided. "But only because I'm going after those two killers as a *civilian* and I may need some expense money if they have gone far from Denver. I'll use what it takes, and I'll return the rest to you."

She shook her head. "Keep the money for your services. We are all due our wages no matter what our task. Just send me their *ears*."

"You want their ears?"

"And their *balls*."

Longarm was accustomed to some strange requests in his line of work, but never had anyone asked him for such disgusting proof of death.

"I can't do that!"

"Sure you can," Maggie countered. "Just cut them off, put them in a box, and mail them to me."

"They'd stink to high heavens. Someone would open the box and then quickly throw it away."

Maggie expelled a long, unhappy sigh. "You're probably right," she agreed. "But at least promise me that you'll kill them slowly and painfully. I heard what they did to Lucy, and I visited the funeral parlor and inspected her poor body. Those men beat her to death and she must have died in agony."

"I'm afraid that she did."

"Then you know what needs to be done," Maggie said. "And I've no doubt that you will do it as we *both* wish."

Maggie Maguire started to leave to take a moment at the casket just before it was lowered into the grave, but Longarm touched her sleeve. "I have a question of some importance."

"Then ask it."

"What about Lucy's brother . . . she said he was a successful banker in Rock Springs, Wyoming."

"Yes, she told me the same thing. Said he was smart and a fine man and that he didn't want anything to do with her and that she should never contact him and sully the Potter name. Lucy mentioned that Horace Potter is also involved in ranching."

"He ought to know about her death."

Maggie frowned. "Why do you think he should know if he never cared about his sister in life?"

"Good question."

"If I were you," Maggie said, "I'd just forget about Mr. Potter. He never needs to know about how badly his sister died."

"But," Longarm countered, "if I had a sister like Lucy, I would want to know when and how she died."

"I don't believe for a moment that he would care," Maggie told him. "But you do as you think best. Personally, I wouldn't bother to raise my skirts and piss in Horace Potter's mouth if he was dying of thirst!"

Longarm had no reply to a statement like that. He stepped away and watched the dirt fly into the grave. When the casket was covered, he took one of the roses he'd bought and laid it at Lucy's head, where the headstone would be placed. He knelt and said, "I'll find them, Lucy. I'll find them and make them wish they had never even been born."

"Custis!"

Longarm turned to see Sarah Freeman hurrying after him. The sharp and disturbing memory of how snooty she'd been when he'd bought poor Lucy a new dress and how she'd looked down on the girl made him keep walking back toward town.

"Custis, please wait!"

He kept walking.

"I'm so sorry! I feel awful for how I treated Miss Potter. Please forgive me!"

Longarm slowed his pace, allowing the woman to overtake him. She slid her arm through his and tried to match his stride. "I . . . I didn't know that she was good," Sarah finally stammered. "I judged her far too harshly and I know that I hurt her feelings. And . . . and if you went to all this expense and trouble, that tells me that she must have been different."

"Different for a whore, you mean?"

"Yes. I suppose that is exactly what I mean."

They were away from the cemetery and only a quarter mile from downtown. Longarm twisted around and glanced back. Maggie and her girls were climbing into a carriage. Only the undertaker remained at the grave site.

"Lucy was badly abused from a very young age. She had no mother and her father was no good. Lucy had an uncle that raped her repeatedly and often long before she should have known that kind of intimacy. Men used her like an animal, but she still had love in her heart. My guess is that her brother was much older and already gone when all the dirtiness happened to his younger sister."

"I . . . I would do *anything* if I could take back the despicable way that I treated Lucy . . . and you."

"Is that right?"

"Of course it is!"

"After you close up your shop late this afternoon, come over to my apartment with a bottle of the best whiskey you can buy," Longarm ordered. "We'll get drunk and go to my bed."

Sarah blinked with shock. "What . . ."

"Sarah, you said you'd do anything, and I want to know if you told the truth."

"Are you going to punish me in your bed? Is *that* what you intend to do?"

"No. I don't hurt women. But I do have a burning anger in me, and maybe with you in bed and enough to drink, it will back off a little."

Sarah swallowed hard. "I'm not at all sure that I can help you, Custis."

"Then don't come," he said, walking away.

Longarm would go straight to his office and turn in his badge after telling Billy Vail he just needed to be free from the shackles of following the law. Billy would, of course, vehemently protest his intentions but Longarm knew he would hold firm.

Thirty minutes later he was in Billy's private office and removing his badge from his person. "Billy, you might as well stop arguing because I'm not changing my mind."

"Do you realize what this could do to your career?"

"Of course I do."

"And what if some local lawman learns that you have taken the law into your own hands and executed those two men? Don't you understand that you could be tried and convicted of *murder*?"

"I know the risks. But first, I have to find Pete and Willie."

"Oh," Billy said, "I've no doubt from the look in your eye that you will do exactly that."

"They deserve a hard death like they gave Lucy."

"And you deserve to bring them to the kind of lawful justice that you've followed since you first came into my office and announced that you wanted to be a United States marshal."

"I've changed a lot since that day."

"Have you really?" Billy asked, studying his face. "I don't believe that for a minute. You still have the same inborn sense of right and wrong. You still believe in our court system of justice . . . not vigilante justice."

"In this case, the only thing that does matter is *real* justice," Longarm argued. "Billy, we've both seen judges and juries make mistakes. What if I have to track that pair of monsters all the way to California? What happens then? I take them to jail and tell some sheriff and judge that they murdered a really fine young woman who just happened to be a whore? How much justice will there be then for Lucy Potter? I'll tell you . . . absolutely none."

Billy leaned over his desk, head down. "I can't stop you from what you have in mind, and I won't even try. Just . . . just never tell me what you did and I'll give you your badge back and the entire thing will be forgotten . . . buried like that young woman was buried this morning."

"Fair enough," Longarm said, smacking his badge down on the desk. "So long, Billy. I'll be back as soon as I can."

"I sure as hell hope so, Custis. I think you'll be back, but what I'm not sure of is what kind of a man you'll be when you return to this office."

"Then that makes two of us," Longarm growled as he left.

Chapter 6

Longarm had just finished cleaning and oiling his weapons when he heard a knock at his door. "Who is it?"

"Sarah."

Longarm let her in. She had a bottle of expensive whiskey in one hand and a hefty package in the other.

"What else did you bring?" he asked as he closed and locked the door behind them.

"Tinned oysters, premium cheeses, sardines, and crackers." She looked at him closely. "I thought we might get a little too drunk to go out to dinner, and I know better than to think I'll get fed here."

He took the whiskey and read the label. "I never could afford this brand so it'll be special. Is it as good as they say?"

"I have no idea because I never wanted to spend the money to find out."

"I'm not only impressed, I'm pleased."

"Good," Sarah said, removing her coat and throwing it

across his old couch. "So let's pour and find out if it was worth nearly ten dollars."

Longarm found a couple of clean glasses and poured. He handed one glass to Sarah and said, "To Lucy Potter, may she rest in peace."

"To Lucy Potter."

They drank and both of them smacked their lips with satisfaction. "It's worth the price," Longarm quickly decided.

"I think so, too."

Lucy took a seat at the small dining room table and studied Longarm for a moment. "I have been wondering why you broke up with me a few months ago. Did you find another companion?"

"No, I was sent to Santa Fe, New Mexico, to track down a pair of train robbers who had taken over five thousand dollars of government bonds. It took me a while."

"You could have told me you were leaving."

"Yeah, but it happened in a hurry."

"Or sent a telegram from Santa Fe."

"I'm sorry."

"Me, too. Why didn't you come around after you returned?"

Longarm shrugged his broad shoulders and felt a rising irritation. "Listen, if the cost of your excellent whiskey and food is that I sit here while you grill me and try to make me feel guilty, then you can pack it all up and walk out my door."

"I'm sorry," she said quietly, draining her glass and then reaching for the bottle to pour a refill. "But you can't really blame me for wondering what I did wrong."

"You didn't do anything wrong," Longarm said, realizing he was being unkind. "I just didn't want to get too involved.

I've told you that I have no plans to get married or raise a family. And you seemed to want to have a husband and children so I just thought it best to part company."

"I see." Lucy came over and sat close to Longarm on the couch. "You know, Custis, people do change in their needs and wants. Women come into my shop one day raving about their perfect husbands . . . and two days later they are ready to kill them and maybe even start looking for someone else."

"What's your point, Sarah?"

"Just that I have been thinking about us for weeks, and maybe I don't want to get married after all."

"Are you just saying that?"

"Yes, but it might be true. And as for children . . . well, to be honest, I am ready to ban them from my dress shop. They come in and start handling the dresses and clothes and usually their hands are filthy and some of them start playing tag or crying or just making a nuisance of themselves. I'm not sure that I like children at all."

"That's interesting and a good sign," Longarm said, only half jesting.

Sarah was quiet for a moment as they both sipped and savored their whiskey. Finally, Sarah said, "It was obvious when you brought Lucy Potter into my shop that you were very taken with her. I was shocked because I knew what she was and she wasn't all that pretty."

"I thought she was quite attractive."

"She looked very sad and very tired," Sarah countered. "Just like most of her kind but . . ."

"But what?"

"She did have a certain quality about her that was different . . . even special. I could see after you two left that there was something going on. Did you make love to her?"

Longarm blinked. "Is that what this has all been leading up to? Did I get the French disease or some other terrible affliction?"

"No!" Sarah cried. "Not at all. You're a smart man. You know women and I know that you would protect yourself, yet . . . yet I couldn't understand why you were with her and not *me*. Was she witty or especially smart?"

"She wasn't particularly smart or witty. But she'd seen the dark side of life and it hadn't ruined her, and that intrigued me. And to answer your first question, I never made love to Lucy."

"I'll bet she wanted you to."

Longarm frowned. "I don't know what she wanted from me," he said truthfully. "We talked and she understood that she needed to get out of the whorehouse but she couldn't see how. I suggested some way might be found."

"What way?"

"I don't know," Longarm answered. "But I thought there was hope and I wanted to help her find respect. Help her find a way to live a good and long life. I could see her dead in a few years the way she was going and I wanted to change that path."

Sarah expelled a long breath and studied the wall. "You wanted to be her salvation. Her protector and redeemer?"

"Maybe I did."

"Well," Sarah mused, "it just means that you have a very good heart, and perhaps somewhere along the line you've done a good woman wrong and thought that this might make amends."

Longarm grinned. "I guess you've analyzed me from my toes to my eyeballs, Sarah. And while I'm not saying there isn't some truth in what you've said, I think it's time we went to bed and do what we do best."

"Cheers," the woman said as she raised and touched his glass in a toast. "Let the fun begin!"

Longarm was on his knees, his big hands cupping both of her breasts. Sarah was on her back with her legs up in the air resting on Longarm's shoulders. Her eyes were glazed with pleasure and half closed, her lips were parted, and her breathing was heavy as he moved in and out of her with increasing speed and intensity.

"Oh . . . oh my gawd!" she moaned as his thrusting became harder and deeper. "Oh, Custis, come on, baby, come on!"

A low, almost animal growl filled Longarm's throat, and he groaned with passion as he strained to give her everything she wanted for the third time that evening. And at last, when her legs began to tremble and a cry burst from her lips, Longarm released his seed. There wasn't a great volume this time, but the pleasure of letting it flow into this woman was so intense that his fingers bit into her lush breasts for an instant and then he collapsed across her body with his hips still pumping furiously.

"Oh, Custis," Sarah gasped when she found her breath. "We're going to kill each other if we don't have some rest. I need whiskey and I need food."

Longarm reared back on his butt and laughed at the ceiling. "And you shall have both! Let's eat and drink again and then see if we can repeat our magnificent performance!"

Sarah grinned and closed her eyes. "It's even better between us than it was before."

"That's because you brought me better whiskey."

She tried to slap him but was just too weak. "Get out of me and let's refresh ourselves because right now I'm worried about being strong enough to get dressed and walk across this bedroom."

"Then don't get dressed and stay right here," he suggested. "I'll bring all the food in on a platter and refresh our drinks."

"I like that idea very much," she whispered. "I feel like my body and my mind are both jelly."

"Raspberry or blackberry?"

"Strawberry," she finally decided. "Go open that tin of oysters and don't forget to bring our crackers and sardines."

"At your service," he told her, hopping naked to the floor, only to discover that his own legs were a little wobbly. He did not know if they would be able to make love again until morning. Sarah had made it very clear that she wasn't going back to her apartment . . . not in the condition she was in and as weak as she felt because of their strenuous lovemaking.

That was fine with Longarm. He had made a mistake to drop this beautiful, passionate woman, but now that mistake had been rectified. Before Sarah left, he would tell her that he had a sworn mission and that was to find and take revenge on Pete and Willie. And that might just take some time. He would not tell her that Maggie Maguire was paying his expenses or that he'd turned in his badge so that he could exact a just vengeance. But he knew that he would send her telegrams while he was on the hunt, and when he returned, he would ask her to bring exactly what she had brought this evening to his apartment . . . both food and her sexual passion.

Chapter 7

Longarm overslept the next morning, and when he rolled out of bed, he realized that Sarah had already arisen to put on fresh underclothes and make herself presentable for her morning customers.

He shaved and dressed and reached into his pants pocket, having forgotten the roll of cash that Maggie Maguire had given him to hunt down Pete and Willie. Longarm frowned, still not sure that he should have accepted the money, but if he had to leave Denver to track down the pair of killers, he needed train fare and expense money. Longarm had never been one to travel on the cheap and so Maggie's funds would be a great help, but he'd return whatever he hadn't spent to bring justice to Lucy.

He stretched, yawned, and then put on his hat and coat, noting that there were dark circles under his eyes because he'd had little sleep. There were also scratches on his back thanks to Sarah's long fingernails and passion; he hoped the fresh scabs would not tear loose and ruin his shirt.

After a few more yawns he headed over to the café, where he usually enjoyed a much earlier breakfast. Only today most of the regular customers had already come and gone so Long-arm took a stool at the counter.

"You look a little drug out this morning," the owner offered, automatically pouring Longarm a cup of strong coffee. "Up all night with a pretty woman playing bumpy and humpy?"

Longarm ignored the crudely phrased question and the man's mischievous grin. "Don't try to be funny this morning, Ed. I'll have the usual ham and eggs, toast, and more coffee."

"Ah, I gather that you are not in the mood for conversation."

Five minutes later Longarm was enjoying his breakfast and downing his second cup of coffee. He raised his cup for a refill. "Didn't mean to be snappy with you this morning," he said by way of an apology. "But yesterday's funeral set me back a little."

"Yeah, I heard you, Maggie, and all her girls were up at the cemetery dressed in black."

"That's right and it was a nice funeral."

"What was Miss Freeman doing there? I can't imagine the whore was one of her customers."

Longarm didn't answer the question. There were times when Ed was a bit too forward and nosy. "You ever serve two fellas named Willie Benton and Pete Rafter?"

"Yeah, a few times. I even hired 'em to do some cleanup work for me once, but they were worthless. Why are you asking?"

"I'd like to find them."

Ed nodded. "Well, I'm afraid that I can't help you but I

do know that they spent quite a bit of time over at the Aspen Stables. They mucked out stalls, fed, and groomed horses in exchange for a place to stay ... especially in the winter when it was too cold to sleep outdoors. I recall Pete telling me that he was a natural with horses and Willie arguing that he was the better horseman. I thought they were both full of shit and I'd tease 'em about the straw in their hair."

"Hmmm," Longarm mused. "I think I'll go over and have a talk with the owner, whose name I once knew but forgot."

"Jonas Reed. He's a strange duck and I think he's spent some time in prison for horse thieving. He's not a talker, that's for sure, and I've never seen a smile on his face."

"So Jonas Reed is cantankerous?"

"Yeah, that's a good way to describe him. He's big, strong, and rough as a cob; I sure wouldn't want to cross the man."

The café owner was short, fat, and he reminded Longarm of a butterball or a jelly roll. It was impossible to imagine Ed fighting anyone, much less winning the fight. "Does Jonas live at his stable?"

"Sure does. He rarely leaves it and I understand that he has some pretty good rental horses. I've seen a few and they're well fed and groomed, so despite what shortcomings the man has, he does love his horses and mules."

Longarm finished his third cup of coffee and paid his bill. He climbed off the stool and ambled toward the door. "Thanks for the information, Ed."

"You think ..."

Longarm didn't wait for the question because he already knew what it would be. Ed would ask him if he thought Pete and Willie had anything to do with the murder of a Denver whore. And somehow, just referring to Lucy in that manner made Longarm upset.

The Aspen Stables had been around for years and had a good reputation although Longarm had never rented a horse or a buggy there because he had heard that Jonas Reed was taciturn and opinionated. The stable owner made it abundantly clear that he didn't like Indians, politicians, or Mexicans. Also that he especially didn't like lawmen.

Longarm approached the stables wondering if Pete and Willie might be hiding inside. He would need to take a look and that probably wouldn't set too well with Jonas Reed.

"Well," Longarm said aloud to himself as he entered the big stable barn, "I'll just see if I can get this done without a fight because I sure don't feel up to one this morning."

"Hello!" Longarm called, not seeing Jonas. "Anyone here?"

"Of course I'm here," the stable owner growled, emerging from a large room filled with saddles and other tack. "What the hell do you want, Marshal?"

Longarm decided on the spot that it might be to his advantage to let the man assume he was still wearing a badge. "I'm looking for Pete Rafter and Willie Benton. I understand that they spend a lot of time here."

"Used to," Jonas said, bitterness thick in his voice. "Not anymore and never again. I'll kill those two thievin' sons-ofbitches if I ever come across 'em! Kill 'em with my bare hands."

Jonas looked plenty capable of the task, and Longarm was surprised by the vehemence in his rough voice. "Mind telling me why?"

"They stole from me!" Jonas boomed. "I trusted them . . . helped them all winter so they didn't freeze in the cold and how do they repay me . . . they steal two of my best mounts and saddles! So I want you to hunt them down and kill the horse-thievin' bastards. The hell of it all is that I just can't get away from here with the livestock I have to care for and feed."

"All right," Longarm said, "why don't you tell me where they might have gone?"

"How should I know?" Jonas roared. "If I knew, I'd hire a gunman to go shoot them and bring back my horses and saddles. But I reckon you'll have to do, Lawman."

"I need some direction if I'm going to have any chance of finding them and bringing back your horses and saddles," Longarm told the stableman. "Because right now I haven't any idea where they would go on the run."

"Well, maybe I do and maybe I don't."

Longarm was an inch taller than Jonas Reed but probably twenty pounds lighter. Jonas was all muscle and mad. Longarm had the feeling that, if he said the wrong thing right now, Jonas was going to try to beat him to a pulp just for being a lawman asking questions.

"The thing is," Longarm said in his most reasonable tone of voice, "we both want justice and that means tracking down the pair. You help me find Pete and Willie and then I'll help you. That's the way it works."

Jonas was fuming, but even angry, he could see that what Longarm was saying made sense and he really did want his horses and saddles returned.

"Okay," the man said, going over and sitting down on an empty whiskey keg and taking a deep breath. "They stole a

paint gelding . . . good-lookin' sonofabitch with three colors—
black, white, and brown. Best-lookin' paint you'll see for a
hundred miles around. And they stole a buckskin mare that I
sure did like . . . she wasn't as tall as the paint but she was
flashy and most anyone could ride her so she was rented out
more than any other animal I own. The paint could be a little
bit fractious and—"

"Hold up," Longarm said. "I got the descriptions of the
horses but I need to know where to start looking for Pete
and Willie."

"They probably headed for Rock Springs, Wyoming,"
Jonas said. "A few days ago they told me about a man they
intended to see and about that little whore that was just buried . . . say, is *that* why you're here? To find Pete and Willie
because you think they might have—"

"Congratulations, Jonas, you figured it out," Longarm
said. "Before Lucy died, she told me that it was Pete and
Willie who killed her."

"Well, I'll be damned!" Jonas exclaimed. "So that's why
they went on the run in such a hurry with my best horses."

"That's right," Longarm agreed. "So not only are they
wanted for stealing your horses and saddles . . . but they're
wanted for murder."

"Humph!" Jonas grunted. "I figure my two best horses are
worth a hell of a lot more than Maggie's favorite little whore."

"How do you know that Lucy was her favorite girl?"
Longarm asked.

Jonas was caught off guard and he blushed. "Well . . .
well, if she wasn't, then Maggie wouldn't have made such
a big deal out of the whore getting buried, now would she?"

"I suppose not," Longarm said, deciding that this man

must have been one of Lucy's regular customers and was too small to admit that fact. "Listen, Jonas, we both have the same objective . . . to find and bring Willie and Pete to justice."

"Marshal, were you sweet on Lucy?"

Longarm pretended not to hear the question and asked one of his own. "Why did you mention that they might be headed for Rock Springs?"

"They were drinkin' real hard the last time I saw 'em here. So drunk that I told 'em to get the hell out of my barn and stay away until they got sober. But before they left . . . they said that they knew the whore's brother was a rich banker and rancher in Rock Springs and there was something said about an inheritance."

Longarm blinked. "What kind of an inheritance?"

"Well, as best I could figure, Lucy was due some inheritance from a father back East . . . a hell of a lot of money, in fact. And the brother, the rich banker in Rock Springs, was also due some of that money. So Pete and Willie were thinking that maybe they could take the whore to Rock Springs and demand what was due her and then they'd split her inheritance . . . or maybe take it all."

Longarm leaned against one of the stalls trying to get a handle on what this new information meant. Up until now, he'd thought that Pete and Willie had just been angry about having to give up money and a pocket knife, but now . . . now deeper motives might be involved, concerning the issue of an inheritance. "Lucy told me her brother's name was Horace Potter and that he was so ashamed of her that they hadn't been in touch for years."

"Can you blame him?" Jonas asked. "Why, it would ruin

a man like that in a town like Rock Springs if the people learned that his sister was a whore. Now that Lucy is buried, the brother is probably celebrating . . . especially if he stands to get a lot more inheritance money."

"You might be right about that," Longarm said, more to himself than to Jonas. "And maybe because Lucy was a prostitute, she was going to be used by Pete and Willie as a threat to get money from the banker."

Jonas shook his big, shaggy head. "It all adds up but makes no difference to me. All I want is what was stolen."

"I'll do my best to return your property."

"Then you're goin' to Rock Springs?"

"I am."

"When?"

Longarm pulled out his railroad pocket watch and consulted it in the dim and cavernous barn. "The Denver Pacific leaves this afternoon at four o'clock, and I'll take it the hundred and six miles north to Cheyenne. This evening, I might be able to get a seat on the Union Pacific. If I do, I'll be in Rock Springs tomorrow afternoon. Pete and Willie can't ride that far that fast so I'll be waiting for them if they show up looking to squeeze Horace Potter for money."

"If they ride into Rock Springs, my paint gelding will stand out from the crowd. When you see that horse, you've by gawd found 'em. I want those horses back!"

"And if I do get them back," Longarm said, "are you going to pay for them to be shipped to Denver?"

"What?"

"You heard me," Longarm said. "I'm sure as hell not going to spend a week or two riding one of them and ponying the other all the way back here to your stable. I'll be riding the train back to Denver."

"Well, hell's fire!" Jonas roared. "You're the damn law and it's your job to find and return what was stolen!"

"Jonas, you're in for a surprise and I might as well give it to you straight. I've handed over my badge. I'm no more the law than you are now."

"What?"

"You heard me. I resigned so I could find and kill Pete and Willie for the savage beating that resulted in Lucy Potter's death."

The big stableman stared at him for a full minute then said, "If you find them and my horses, you'd better not come back to this town without 'em. Hear me?"

"Yeah, I hear you," Longarm said, trying to tamp down his anger. "You've had your loss and I've had mine. If you want those horses back, you're going to have to either pay for it or do it yourself."

Jonas began to shake with fury. His big fists doubled up and Longarm knew that the man was getting ready to start a fight.

"Don't," Longarm said quietly, his hand flashing in a cross draw that brought his big Colt revolver pointing an inch away from Jonas's heart. "Don't even think about throwing a punch, because before it starts, you'll have a bullet in your brisket."

The giant seemed to teeter between reason and insanity, but then his lips split into a cold grin. "If you plan to come back here, you'd best bring my horses, mister."

"I'll keep that in mind," Longarm told him as he turned and left the man.

"You should kill 'em *slow*! Put a rope around their necks and hoist 'em both up stranglin' instead of droppin' them hard so their necks break!"

"I'll keep that in mind!" Longarm shouted back over his shoulder into the dark, fetid barn.

Longarm had a lot to do in a hurry if he wanted to catch that northbound train to Cheyenne. He'd tell Sarah and Billy what he'd learned and then start the manhunt.

Chapter 8

Pete and Willie reined their stolen horses up at sundown and stared at the little homestead about a mile away. It was getting chilly and they were still a good distance south of Laramie. They had figured that someone might come after them and their horses and so they'd cut directly northwest to avoid Cheyenne and head straight up to Laramie and then turn east and ride over to Rock Springs. But now, they were bone tired and their horses were played out. They had no food, thin blankets, and the night ahead was going to be cold.

"We'll hole up at that cabin," Pete decided, watching wood smoke curl into the salmon-colored sky. "Maybe stay a day or two and rest these horses. We've been traveling too fast and hard."

"Do you think that Jonas will be comin' after us?"

"I hope not," Pete worried. "He'd be a hell-dog in a fight but I don't see how he could leave his business to give chase. Still, he'd be a bad man to tangle with."

"Yeah, but it don't matter how big and strong Jonas is," Willie said, patting the gun on his hip. "Ain't no man can stand up to fight after I put a bullet through his damned heart."

"Well," Pete said, "the last time we shot at anything, I seem to recall that neither one of us could hardly hit the side of a barn."

"We were drunk!" Willie argued. "I'm not all that bad a shot."

"The hell you say." Pete drew rein and pointed to a tree. "Show me if you can hit it from here. It's about the same size around as Jonas."

"By gawd, I can hit it easy!" Willie bragged, drawing his gun with his right hand and wrapping his reins around his saddle horn with his left. "I can drill it dead damned center!"

"Shoot the gun and not your mouth," Pete said, tightening his reins on the paint horse. "I'm waitin' to see if your brag stands up."

Willie raised his pistol, took a quick aim, and fired. His bullet *did* strike the big pine but neither man noticed because the buckskin mare that Willie was astraddle was so startled by the shot that it began to buck. Willie sailed high over the mare's head and landed so hard on his back that his trigger finger jerked off another shot up into the sky. The mare kept bucking for about twenty yards then stopped and looked around, every bit as surprised by what had just happened as the man who had been riding her.

"Gawdamn!" Willie cried, groaning in pain. "I think maybe I broke my right shoulder!"

Pete was not a sympathetic man. "Anybody ought to know you don't shoot off a horse you don't know a damn thing about!"

"Well, you sure didn't say anything about her maybe buckin'!" Willie moaned as he struggled to his knees then his feet. He raised his gun, determined to shoot hot lead up the buckskin mare's ass.

"No!" Pete shouted, spurring his paint in between his partner and the valuable buckskin mare. "What the hell is wrong with you? Did you land on your head and go stupid? You shoot that horse and you'll by gawd walk all the way to Laramie!"

Willie reluctantly lowered his gun. "Damn, my shoulder hurts. I sure as hell broke it maybe a couple of places." He gritted his teeth in pain. "I need a doctor, Pete. I need one real bad!"

"Well, at least you hit the tree you aimed at," Pete said, dismounting and leading the paint over to collect the spooked buckskin. "Easy, now," he crooned, hoping the mare wouldn't bolt and run away. "Easy, girl."

Pete took hold of the mare's bit and gently lifted her reins over her head. He led the buckskin back to Willie and handed him the reins. "Maybe that cabin yonder will have whiskey. We could both sure as hell use a good drink tonight."

"Yeah, but I need a *doctor*!"

"You'll be damned lucky to get food, a bed, and a bottle," Pete roughly countered. "I got no time for stupidity, Willie. We got to get to Rock Springs and see if we can get that money off Lucy's rich brother."

"What about my broken shoulder, you heartless sonofabitch!" Willie raged. "I'm in *terrible* pain!"

"I can't help that for now. It's getting dark fast and I sure hope whoever is living in that cabin up yonder didn't hear your foolish gunshot. If they did, we might be in trouble showing up at this late evening hour."

"I'll kill for whiskey," Willie whimpered. "I mean it, Pete. I ain't ridin' past that cabin. That's where we're stayin' the night."

"Suits me. Maybe there are women in that cabin. Wife and a pretty young daughter and some good hot stew and whiskey. Now wouldn't that be fine?"

"Yeah, it would be," Willie eagerly agreed. "And I'll tell you something else. Soon as I can, I'm going to sell this mare and find a better horse to ride. One that I can trust not to half kill me."

"You shouldn't have shot off her. You should have gotten down first and learned what she'd do when a gun was fired next to her ear."

"Well, you didn't say anything about it so shut your yap, Pete! I can't take your carping right now. This buckskin bitch damned near tossed me into a funeral parlor."

"Yeah," Pete said, "you got tossed so high I was lookin' to see if Saint Peter had whittled his initials in the soles of your boots."

"Just shut up, and hold the mare tight while I try to climb on. I sure wish I'd have landed on my left shoulder instead of my right."

"Me, too! With your right shoulder broke, you're goin' to be about as useless as tits on a boar hog when we get to Rock Springs."

"I'll carry my water, don't you worry about that," Willie grunted as he managed to hoist himself back in the saddle. "And I sure wish I could put a bullet between this mare's ears."

"Don't do it. When we get to Laramie, we can sell her for a good price and buy you an old plow horse or mule to ride so you don't get tossed again."

"I ain't ridin' a damn mule!"

But Pete wasn't listening. He'd seen lights go on through the cabin's windows and felt a cold breeze coming off the mountains. He sure hoped there was food, women, and whiskey waiting just up ahead, and he knew that if killing had to be done to get what they needed for this night, then killing they would do.

"Hello the house!" Pete shouted when they drew near the big log cabin. "Anybody home?"

"Of course there's somebody home!" Willie hissed with a grimace on his face. "Let's just unload our carcasses and go on inside."

"Yeah, and what if there's a man waitin' behind the door to blow us all to hell with a double-barreled shotgun?"

Willie didn't have an answer to the question so after a few moments, Pete yelled, "Got a man hurt real bad here and we could use some help!"

The door cracked open and a quarter of a body and face peeked around the corner. "Who are you and what is your business?"

"We're travelin' up to Laramie."

"Well," the man behind the door replied, "you got a ways to ride yet so I suggest you keep movin'."

"But my friend broke his shoulder!"

"Yeah," Willie wailed, "and I'm in a lot of pain. You got some whiskey and food?"

The man behind the door emerged holding a pistol pointed at the two arrivals. "I don't trust strangers . . . especially a pair that look as rough as you fellas."

"Christian charity," Pete said, wondering if he and Willie were going to have to ride off, tie their horses, and then lay siege to the cabin until they either killed this asshole or he decided to finally show some charity.

"Get off your horses and tie 'em at the rail," the home-steader reluctantly decided. "Then step up here with your hands where I can see them plainly."

Pete was getting angry. "You sure are a suspicious feller."

"I've got reason to be careful with a wife and a couple of small children in here. Now you fellas do as I say or ride on to Laramie. I'm of no mind to trifle with problems other than my own."

Pete glanced at Willie and whispered, "First chance we get, let's kill him."

"I already decided as much," Willie whispered back. "Now help me down from this accursed mare."

Pete got his partner down and they led their horses close to the cabin. For just an instant, they saw a pretty yellow-haired woman's face in the lone front window.

"That's far enough," the homesteader ordered. "What do you require?"

"Food and a couple of blankets would be appreciated," Pete said.

"And whiskey," Willie quickly added. "I'm in a hell of a lot of pain from this broke shoulder."

"You don't look too good, that's for sure," the home-steader said. "But then neither does your friend."

"We ain't standin' here in the dark to be insulted, mister."

The man turned slightly because his wife was speaking, but Pete noticed the barrel of his gun didn't waver during the short conversation. After a few moments, the home-steader said, "I won't let strangers into the house but you can go to the barn and take shelter. There's some grain and grass hay for those horses. They look like they've been ridden hard."

"Is that the best you can do?" Willie said angrily. "Mister, I'm in a lot of pain and I sure could use some whiskey."

The homesteader considered the request and somewhere behind him his yellow-haired wife was talking. Finally, the homesteader relented. "You men go to the barn and unsaddle. Feed and water your horses and I'll be along with some food and a little whiskey."

"You sayin' we'll be eating in your *barn*?" Willie asked, feigning shock as if he'd been accustomed to eating on clean table linen.

"That's right. You can sleep in the straw and there are a few old saddle blankets you can use to keep warm. It's the best that I will offer two rough strangers who show up at night."

Willie started to say that what was offered wasn't much but Pete spoke first. "Well, if that's the way it is to be, then that's the way we'll do it."

"Don't shit in my barn," the homesteader warned. "Nor piss. I'll be along with a couple of plates and a little whiskey. If it wasn't for the missus jawin' at me now, I'd send you packing in a helluva hurry."

"You ain't the kindest man I ever come across," Pete grumped. "But we'll take what we can get of your help."

"It might be more than either of you rough-looking fellas deserve," the man said as he closed the door.

Pete and Willie both heard a crossbar slide into place, and they turned and started walking toward the barn. Willie was furious. "I can't believe how shabby he treated us and what he said about how we looked. I'm going to shoot him when he comes out with the food and whiskey then I'm going to kill his whole damned family."

"Just . . . just simmer down a bit," Pete warned. "We'll

shoot him and then we'll take what we need, but I see no good to come of killing a woman and a couple of kids. Rape her, sure, but not kill her. Understand?"

"We accidentally killed Lucy."

"She was a whore. This is different."

Willie shrugged. Truth be known, he was in such pain, he had no interest in raping a woman this night. He just wanted the pain to stop, and whiskey would help until they got to Laramie and a doctor.

Both men entered the dark barn and found a lantern. They looked around and saw the grass hay and a few sacks of grain. "I'll unsaddle and feed our horses. You hide right behind the barn door and shoot the husband when he comes close."

"My pleasure," Willie said. "But my aim is gonna be a little shaky because I'll be shooting with the wrong hand."

"Then don't shoot until he's up so close you can't miss," Pete advised. "But kill him on the spot because I got a feeling once we take a shot at him, he's going to shoot back. From what little I've seen, he's a tough man."

"No," Willie countered, "he's a *dead* man."

Thirty minutes had passed and the homesteader hadn't appeared with the food and whiskey. Pete and Willie were getting more impatient and angry by the second. "Damn!" Pete hissed. "What in the hell is takin' him so long?"

"Damned if I know," Willie said, looking like he was ready to burst into tears because he was hurting so badly. "But if the sonofabitch doesn't show up quick, I'm going to go up to that cabin and shoot everyone inside! We don't deserve to be treated so poorly."

"You're right," Pete agreed. "And—"

"Freeze!" the homesteader yelled from behind them as

he slipped through a small opening in the back of the barn. "Drop your gun or I'll kill you both!"

Pete and Willie whirled around and there he was with a big shotgun in his fists. The homesteader was a bull of a man, just under six feet tall and wide in the shoulders. He stood in the darkest shadows but there was no mistaking the clicks of two hammers on a double-barreled shotgun. Willie dropped his gun. Pete almost dropped a load in his pants.

The homesteader advanced with the shotgun trained on their bodies. "I knew you two were pure poison," the man said. "I can read dishonesty just as plain as I can read the pages of a book."

Neither Pete nor Willie knew what to say. No doubt the homesteader had been listening to the last part of their conversation. Maybe, they both thought, it was *their* time to die.

Finally, Pete managed to say, "What are you going to do to us?"

"I'm thinking on that right now."

"Maybe . . . maybe you should just let us resaddle our horses and ride away," Willie said hopefully.

"So you can steal back here in the night and try to kill me and my family?"

"No sir! We'd not do that," Pete said fervently. "Not your family. You'd never see us again."

"Then you'd try to kill some other good family in this wide open and sparsely settled country," the homesteader said. "That's exactly what you'd do."

"No sir!" Pete said again. "We . . . we'd just ride on to Laramie and be gone."

The homesteader came nearer. He was a man in his late twenties, handsome with a strong jaw and a low, menacing brow.

"I ought to kill you right now," he hissed. "Everything inside tells me you are both wicked disciples of Satan. But I can't do that so I'm letting you go free."

"Well, thank you!"

"On foot," the homesteader said. "Without your weapons."

Willie began to shake his head. "You . . . you can't be serious, mister! It's probably fifty miles to Laramie and it's real cold out there."

"More like sixty miles," the homesteader said with a cold smile. "Now grab your saddlebags and head outside. I'm going to follow you for a mile or two and then you're on your own. I'd advise you to walk fast and follow the North Star."

"Oh, mister," Willie begged, "show us a little Christian kindness on this cold, dark night!"

"You were going to kill me and my family . . . after you raped my wife."

"No!" Willie cried in protest. "I'm in so much pain I couldn't rape anything tonight! I swear that's the truth."

"You wouldn't know the truth if it punched you in the mouth," the man scoffed. "Now untie your saddlebags and head for the door before I change my mind and kill both of you treacherous bastards!"

Pete looked at Willie and shook his head. "Looks like we drew a bad hand this time around. No sense in making it even worse by dyin'."

"You mean you're going to let this man steal our horses, saddles, guns, and rifles?"

"We have no choice but to do that," Pete said.

Tears of anger, mixed with pain and pure frustration, began to stream down Willie Benton's dirty face. But when

Pete untied his saddlebags and tossed his pistol on the floor of the barn, Willie knew he had to do the same or he was a dead man.

Someday, he silently vowed, *I will return and kill this family then rob them and burn everything they owned to the gawdamn ground!*

Chapter 9

After arriving in Cheyenne on the Denver Pacific Railroad, Longarm had a few hours to kill until the westbound Union Pacific rolled into the train station. It was almost sundown and he figured he ought to get a good steak before leaving. The wind was blowing hard as it most often did in Cheyenne, and the smell of the stockyards filled the early evening air.

Despite the wind, Longarm had always liked Cheyenne even though he would be the first to admit that it was not the most picturesque town in Wyoming. It was big, flat, and wide open, and most of the town relied upon either the railroad or the ranches for their livelihood. As in many railroad towns, there were one hell of a lot of saloons and they were never quiet or empty.

As Longarm carried his travel bag from the railroad station up the main street of town, he wondered if there was any chance that Pete and Willie had somehow managed to arrive here first. Longarm just didn't see how that might be possible, but he still kept his eye out for a paint gelding and a pretty buckskin mare tied to some hitching rail. If the pair of killers were here, he'd save himself a lot of time and trouble and Maggie Maguire a lot of money. And he itched to see them suffer for the terrible act they had committed.

"Evening," he said to a couple walking arm in arm along the uneven boardwalk.

"And a fine evening it is," the man said, offering a broad smile.

Longarm approached the sheriff's office and decided he owed Sheriff George Gibson a quick visit. Gibson was a good man and he'd been helpful to Longarm in the past. Maybe he would prove to be a real help in locating Pete and Willie.

"Hello," he said, opening the door and finding the sheriff still at his desk. "Isn't it time that you locked up and went home?"

Sheriff Gibson was in his fifties, but looked a few years older. He was a tough man, but had the reputation of being scrupulously honest and always fair. He wasn't tall or even particularly strong looking, but he had steely gray eyes and a prominent jaw that gave evidence that he was a man not to be trifled with. For years, he'd successfully handled the rough-and-ready local cowboys and the equally contentious railroad workers they usually fought with. Both sides thought that Sheriff Gibson liked them the best, and that in itself was a testament to how well he handled the streets and the daily quarrels.

"Well, I'd like to go but my best deputy quit a few days ago for a sheriff's badge in Rock Springs," Gibson explained, sticking out his hand. "Can't blame him because the pay was twenty dollars more a month."

"Would that be Dub Turner?"

"Yeah," the sheriff said. "Dub is probably tough enough to survive over in Rock Springs, but it won't be easy. That town has had a string of sheriffs and none of them lasted more than a few months. They either get shot, beaten up, or fired. There is a helluva lot of fighting, feuding, and politics in Rock Springs. I wouldn't take that job for twice what they've started Dub at, but he was tired of being the second dog in this office so he decided to move on. We parted on good terms and I wished him luck and told him that, if the job didn't work out, I'd hold his job open a month before I started looking for his replacement."

"I might be spending a little time in Rock Springs," Longarm said, taking an empty chair.

Gibson kicked his heels up on his desk, laced his fingers behind his head, and asked, "And why the hell would you do a thing like that?"

"Well, it's a long and kind of complicated story, George. How about you lock this place up for the night and I'll buy you a steak and a whiskey and tell you what I'm up to."

"Sounds like the best offer I've had all day," Gibson said, grinning. "As long as you're buying."

"I am," Longarm promised.

"They pay United States marshals much better than they do local sheriffs, and that's for sure. At least I won't feel guilty."

"You could always get a hold of my boss, Billy Vail, and see about pinning on a federal badge. Right now he's short one good man."

"That a fact?" Gibson asked, looking only mildly interested.

"It is," Longarm said, "because I just resigned."

The sheriff dropped his boots to the ground and stared at Longarm. *"What?"*

"It's not permanent," Longarm assured the man, "but

there's some retribution that I have to do and I don't want to be held back by the law."

"I can't believe that I'm hearing you say this. I hope you're going to explain everything over a nice juicy steak."

"That's my intention."

"Let's get going! I assume since you're carrying that bag that you're planning on catching the next train westbound."

"As always, you're very observant."

"I never miss much," the sheriff of Cheyenne agreed as they headed out for a good steak.

"So," Gibson said as they enjoyed their steaks, "you think that this prostitute you befriended might have been chosen by the pair that beat her to death."

"Yes."

"And they did it because she was dumb enough to tell them about some inheritance that she thought she had coming?"

"Lucy Potter was someone I liked, but I never said she was real smart."

"Were you payin' her for her favors?"

"Hell no!" Longarm protested. "I was just trying to help her out. Maybe get her straight. She had—"

"Let me guess." Gibson chuckled. "She had long, pretty legs, big tits, and she could make a man like you pant like a dog in the summer sun."

"Damn, George, it wasn't like that at all."

"Well, then, what was it?"

"I told you," Longarm said a little gruffly. "First time I saw her was along Cherry Creek and she was getting beat up by Pete Rafter and Willie Benton. I couldn't let that pass so I helped her out. Then when I heard her story, I sort of got involved."

"And she got killed."

"Yeah, and unfortunately it wasn't quick or easy," Longarm said. "I mean to exact some serious punishment on that pair when I find them. Maybe even kill them if there is any excuse at all."

"Don't just gun them down in cold blood or you'll be the one going to prison or to the gallows," Gibson warned around a mouthful of steak. "I sure wouldn't want to have to arrest you in my town, and I doubt any other sheriff would either."

"I'll be careful," Longarm promised. "But I'm not going to stop until I find and bring them to a painful justice. They're both bad to the bone, George. They need to either be pushing up flowers or rotting in prison, and I think that I'd be doing mankind a big favor if I shot them dead."

"I see," the sheriff said. "But I sure hate to hear that you've handed over your badge, Custis."

"It was necessary."

"So what's your plan? Are you going to go to Rock Springs and just hang around hoping the pair turn up?"

"I don't have any idea of what else to do." Longarm took a sip of the good red wine he'd ordered. "And there is the matter of Horace Potter that needs some close looking at and my attention."

"You don't think a man as successful as Potter would have anything to do with having his own sister killed, do you?"

"Probably not," Longarm was forced to agree. "But think about this, George. With his sister dead, if there really is some inheritance, Horace would get all or most of it. And he wouldn't have to worry anymore about Lucy showing up unexpectedly and putting his social standing in Rock Springs at risk. Apparently, Horace actually owns a bank there and—"

"I've heard of the man," George Gibson interrupted. "All bad."

"What?"

"He's known for making loans to businesses, small ranchers, and homesteaders that he knows can't meet the terms of the loans then foreclosing on them and taking their properties for a song. I've heard about him doing that for years. I've also heard that he just about runs the town . . . or at least he stands in the background and pulls the strings that make the elected officials dance."

"And on top of all that, he owns a ranch?" Longarm asked.

"That's right. A pretty big one although the name of it escapes me at the moment." Gibson took a drink of wine. "What I'm trying to tell you is that Horace Potter is a ruthless sonofabitch who has the money and political connections to pretty much do what he wants to do in Rock Springs. And that means that you had damn sure better tread lightly when you go to his office and start asking questions about his dead sister and maybe him having some connection to her death in order to get a bigger inheritance."

"I see." Longarm shook his head. "Looks like I'm going to land in a hornet's nest the minute I step off the train in Rock Springs."

"I'd say so."

"Will your former deputy, now the new sheriff in Rock Springs, help and stand by me?"

"Probably not," George said after a long pause. "Dub knew

what he was getting into when he took the job. And guess who one of the men who interviewed him for the job was?"

"Horace Potter."

"That's right. And although I only saw Dub for a few hours after he returned here to resign and clean up some business, he said enough to me so that I understood what kind of game he was getting into. I offered him five dollars more a month if he stayed because he was a damned good deputy, but he wanted to be top dog in Rock Springs and so I wished him well."

"Is he honest?" Longarm asked, needing to make sure.

"When Dub left here to take that sheriff's job, he was honest . . . but I don't know if he could hold on to that in such a situation. Dub was a good man, but he was real ambitious and I think he had bigger fish to fry than always wearing a badge. I got the impression that he thought he had a very bright and prosperous future in Rock Springs."

Longarm took all of this in, and it didn't sound good. He needed an ally in Rock Springs, and if newly appointed Dub Turner had slid over to the shady side of life, then that would only make things all that much more difficult.

"I'll keep my eyes peeled for that paint and buckskin," Gibson offered as the apple pie was brought over to their table.

"I appreciate that," Longarm told his old friend. "But even though Pete and Willie aren't the brightest pair I've ever come across, I don't think they're stupid enough to ride straight up here from Denver. They'd have to know that I'd be looking for them as well as out to retrieve the horses that were stolen from the Aspen Stables."

"Jonas Reed's horses, huh?"

"That's right."

"My oh my," Gibson said. "I can't believe that he isn't either dead or in prison. Jonas is one violent and quick-on-the-trigger sonofabitch. I'm surprised that he didn't come after that pair himself."

"He runs a good business and owns a lot of horses and mules to take care of," Longarm explained. "But we had some words, and it was clear that he wanted to go on the hunt for Pete and Willie."

"I had a run-in with Jonas years ago when he came through here and I was a new deputy. I knew that I sure wasn't a big and tough enough man to whip him in a fistfight so I waited until he was dead drunk and then I pistol-whipped him good and it took two men to drag him into jail. When he woke up the next morning, Jonas was so gawdamn mad I thought he might tear the bars out of the cell and bend them around our necks. The judge let him leave Cheyenne without a fine but only on the condition that he never set foot in this town again."

"That sounds like him and he hasn't changed much with age," Longarm said, coming to his feet after hearing the train whistle blow. "George, as always, it's been a pleasure to visit with you."

"Same goes here," Gibson said. "And be sure to check with the telegraph office now and then in Rock Springs. If I come across that pair, I'll get a message to you right after I arrest them."

"They're killers and they're sneaky," Longarm warned. "If you brace them, make sure that you do it on your terms."

"Always, Custis. Always."

Longarm shook the man's hand, paid for their meals . . . or rather Maggie Maguire did . . . and headed for the train station.

Chapter 10

The two cold, shivering men were staggering with weariness when the sun broke over the eastern hills, but Laramie was still too far north to be seen. Pete Rafter was sick and tired of his friend Willie's constant whining, groaning, and moaning about his broken right shoulder. The man wasn't going to be a damn bit of help when it came down to getting money out of Mr. Horace Potter in Rock Springs.

No help at all.

He's going to be the death of me, Pete told himself over and over. *He almost got us killed back at that homestead and he's going to do it for certain when we get to Laramie or Rock Springs. I have to get rid of the sonofabitch and I have to do it soon. Willie is more interested in getting guns and killing that homesteader and his family than he is in us finally making a lot of money. He ain't thinking straight anymore . . . if he ever did at all.*

Even as Pete considered what had to be done, he shied away from actually doing it. He and Willie had been through thick and thin for the past five years, and while they'd argued almost constantly, they'd also committed a lot of successful crimes together and neither one had even considered turning the other in to the law for a reward.

Willie was dumb, but he was trustworthy, brave, and not afraid of anyone or anything. He wasn't good with a gun, but he was a damned tough fighter and he was good with a knife and as a pickpocket. But they'd crossed the line regarding small crimes. They'd beaten Lucy Potter to death, and now they were also wanted for horse thieving . . . both hanging offenses.

Willie is going to get my neck stretched, Pete had reminded himself over and over through the long, freezing cold night. *I got to kill him before Laramie is in our sights.*

Pete was so cold he couldn't stop shaking, and when Willie collapsed and curled into a ball to try and get warmer, Pete knew that he needed to take care of business.

"You go on to Laramie," Willie begged, teeth chattering. "Steal us horses and guns and come back for me. I can't walk no farther."

Pete started to argue, but then shut his mouth for a moment before sighing deeply and saying, "You're quitting, huh?"

"I can't go a step farther, damn you!"

"I understand."

"I feel so bad I could die." Willie looked up at his friend with cold tears leaking out of the corners of his eyes. "Get us horses, whiskey, and guns. I'll see a doctor in Laramie, and then we'll ride back to that homestead and kill them all! Burn the house and barn to the ground . . . and rape the females. Make them suffer like I'm suffering."

"And what about Rock Springs and all that money we been planning to get from Lucy's rich brother?"

"That can wait!" Willie cried. "We got some payback to do!"

"Okay." Pete removed his coat and laid it over Willie. "Just go to sleep for a while. I'll push for Laramie and come back as soon as I can."

Willie nodded, trying to keep himself from crying. "We always helped each other when it came time. I never had a better friend than you, Pete."

"Me neither, Willie. I'll see you on the other side."

"What other side?" Willie barely managed to ask.

"Of the tracks," Pete said after a moment. "The *railroad tracks* is what I meant."

"Hurry on now, Pete! I need a doctor and something for this pain."

"I know you do. I'm going to help you out."

Willie closed his eyes. Pete walked off a ways to a rocky outcropping and hefted several rocks before deciding on one that was round and probably weighed ten pounds. He wiped the dirt off it and sat down to watch the sun come fully up on the eastern horizon. The air was still very cold but now Pete's mind was just as cold. He waited a few more minutes and then he heard Willie Benton's snoring.

He's going to get me hanged if I don't kill him now.

Pete's big fingers squeezed hard on the rock. He walked back to his sleeping companion and knelt at the man's side. *He stinks just like a pig or a goat. Willie hated to take a bath and I never grew used to his stench. Poor, dumb bastard.*

Pete raised the rock high up in the air and then brought it down on Willie's face just as hard as he possibly could.

Willie screamed. Pete hit him again, smashing his face to pulp. Willie shuddered, blood poured out of his eyes, nose, and what was hardly recognizable as his mouth.

Pete brought the rock down once more with all the power that remained in his body.

Willie's feet danced on the cold, hard ground, bloody bubbles formed on his lips, and then he shuddered and was dead still.

I sure do wish it had worked out for us, pardner. But a man has to take care of himself first . . . we always agreed on that much. By noon, the buzzards will have found you and soon after coyotes and varmints. I gave you death in your sleep, and that's probably a better death than I'll ever have for myself.

So long, Willie, it's been good to know you. I'll meet you on the other side in Satan's burning hell.

Chapter 11

Late that evening Longarm dozed off in the smoking car and didn't awaken until the Union Pacific stopped for wood and water in Laramie. He had elected not to pay extra for a sleeping car between Cheyenne and Rock Springs, figuring that after a big steak dinner and a few drinks, he would sleep well in the coach's nice, comfortable chairs.

"Excuse me," a voice said along with a tug at his coat sleeve. "Is this seat taken?"

Longarm roused awake just long enough to nod and then fall back asleep. When the sun came up the next day, it was chasing them into the small railroad stop known as Rawlins. Longarm stretched and gazed out at the flat, sage-covered country, which seemed better suited to raising sheep or jackrabbits than cattle. He yawned and then realized that someone had taken the seat next to him, making it impossible to get up and go to the toilet.

And that person was quite an attractive woman who was fast asleep.

"Ma'am," he said after a few minutes and realizing that he desperately needed to take a piss, "I'm sorry to wake you but I need to get up and moving."

She opened her eyes, blinked, and then started a little when she saw Longarm's face only inches from her own. "Oh, I'm sorry!"

The woman quickly left her seat, and when Longarm climbed past her into the aisle, he realized that this car was packed and every seat had been taken . . . many by soldiers from Fort Steele. Most of the soldiers and other passengers were still sleeping, and Longarm didn't have to wait in a line to do his personal business. When he returned to his seat, the woman was gone.

"Probably to the dining car," Longarm mumbled to himself. "She'd be more comfortable there than crowded in with rough strangers like myself."

Having nothing better to do and needing coffee to revive, Longarm made his way to the dining car and found the woman sitting all by herself and gazing out the window.

"May I join you?" Longarm asked.

She nodded and tried but failed at a smile. Longarm sat down and signaled for a pot of coffee.

He waited until his coffee arrived, then asked, "Going far?"

"My long journey is almost over," she said. "I've come a great distance to reach Rock Springs."

"That's where I'm going as well."

"Have you been there before?"

"I don't want to be the bearer of bad news, but Rock Springs isn't all that much to talk about. It never really grew like Cheyenne or Reno."

"I've heard that said a few times since I left Charleston."

"You *have* come a long way," he remarked.

"Have you ever been to Charleston?"

"I have," Longarm said. "I was there during the tragic War Between the States."

"Terrible war," she said, shaking her head. "And I was right when I thought I heard just the trace of the South in your voice."

"Very few people even mention that after so many years living in the West."

"Do you live in Wyoming?" she asked.

"Denver, Colorado."

"I've heard nothing but good things about Denver. I should like to visit there someday."

"If you do," Longarm said, "I'd be happy to show you around if you are so inclined to have company."

"How nice of you," she replied, turning to stare out the window. "Does much of the American West look like *this*?"

The way that she said "this" told Longarm that the woman found this part of Wyoming far less than picturesque.

"It's very different all over the West," he began. "In Colorado, Wyoming, and Montana we have the Rocky Mountains, and they are far more impressive than the mountains you are used to back in the East."

"Yes, it was dark when we rolled over the Laramie Mountains, but from what I could see, they were very tall and beautiful. Are the Rockies even taller?"

"Much taller and more extensive. And then in California you have the Sierra Nevada Mountains, which are pretty impressive by anyone's standards. And in between, there are vast deserts with salt and alkali flats."

"Coming from the South, I doubt I'd like the deserts at

all. Is this what they look like?" she asked, pointing toward the window and the country.

"They look far drier, and many have cactus."

"Yes, I've heard of cactus and they're mostly found in the Arizona Territory."

"That's right." Longarm was impressed. "It seems that you must have done some reading before you started this long journey from the South."

"I did," she admitted. "I love the lore of cowboys, Indians, gunfighters, desperadoes, and brave sheriffs! I've even read some of those thrilling dime novels that are so popular back in the East."

Longarm chuckled. "I've read one or two, and they are pretty . . . well, they sensationalize and romanticize the West. In truth, it is beautiful out here, but most people live ordinary lives without a lot of excitement."

"I'm sure that's true, but you have a lot of colorful characters. I've already had talks with some cowboys and other rough types on this train and I'll have to say this . . . they are quite virile and direct in their thinking and the way they go about their lives. However, they all treated me with great respect."

"There were a lot of soldiers in the coach this morning. I'm sure that any of them would give a month's pay just to talk to you."

"I'm really not that interesting," she replied.

"Interesting or not," Longarm replied, "you are very attractive, and there aren't nearly as many women out in the West as there are men . . . most of whom are bachelors."

"Oh," she said with a shy smile, "I understand what you are saying and I'm flattered. But while I'm in Rock Springs, I won't be out and about much. I'll be staying at a real cattle ranch surrounded by thousands of acres. I hope to get a chance to learn how to ride and rope. Are you a cowboy?"

"No," Longarm told her. "I . . . I'm an ex-lawman."

"Oh my!" The woman clapped her hands together. "I'm sure you could tell me many tales!"

"I wouldn't want to shock you with any gory details."

"Then you *have* killed men?"

"Yes, but always in the office of my profession and never with any gladness. Sometimes, very evil men need to be killed for the betterment of society."

"Are they mostly shot . . . or hanged?" she asked, leaning forward with her eyes bright and intense.

"Both," he told her. "But most are killed in saloon fights."

The woman leaned back and studied his face. "Yes, you really do fit the image I had of a fearless and resolute lawman. You're big and strong and have those steely eyes. I think you must have killed many evil men."

"More," he said, sipping his coffee, "than I care to remember."

They both lapsed into an awkward silence that stretched on until Longarm said, "I hope that you find your time at the cattle ranch near Rock Springs to be very interesting and enjoyable, Miss . . ."

"Dunn. Amy Dunn."

"My name is Custis Long."

"Custis is a very manly first name, and it fits you, sir."

"Thank you."

Amy finished her coffee and got up to leave. "It has been nice to meet you, Mr. Long. I hope we meet again and have time to talk some more."

"We have more time right now," Longarm told the woman. "Can I buy you breakfast?"

She hesitated only a moment and then slowly settled back into her seat. "Well, actually that would be very nice. I'm not one to give a false impression, Mr. Long, but—"

"Custis," he corrected. "Please call me by my manly first name."

"As you wish. In truth, I've spent all my funds on this great journey from Charleston. I am almost penniless, but I have someone in Rock Springs who I know will help me."

"The man with the big cattle ranch?"

"That's right. Horace is—"

Longarm almost dropped his cup and spilled coffee all over the table. "You're going there to visit a *Mr. Horace Potter*?"

"However did you know?" she asked in astonishment.

"I've heard a great deal about Horace Potter, the wealthy cattle rancher and bank owner. I'm sure that he is well known throughout this part of Wyoming."

"I suppose so," Amy said. "I'm very proud of my brother."

"He's your *brother*?" Longarm looked closely at her face and realized for the first time that she bore a distinct resemblance to Lucy. Amy was definitely a Potter.

"Why are you staring at me like that all of a sudden?" Amy asked. "Is anything wrong?"

"Not at all," Longarm said, recovering quickly. "It's just that I would have thought that someone related to that man would probably have money and—"

"I'm the late child in the family. By the time I was five, my brother and sister had already left Charleston, Arkansas."

"Arkansas?"

"Yes." Suddenly she laughed. "Of course! You immediately assumed that I was from Charleston, in *West Virginia*.

No, no. Charleston, Arkansas, is a small town not far from Fort Smith. But don't blame yourself for the misunderstanding. It happens quite often."

The waiter reappeared and Longarm ordered a hearty breakfast. Amy did the same. As soon as they were alone, Longarm asked, "So you were a Potter, but married a Mr. Dunn."

"Yes. He was killed two years ago in a railroad accident. My husband was an engineer and died while working on an important but damaged railroad trestle. I receive a small pension, but it's not enough to support me."

Longarm took a deep breath as he thought about Lucy and the reason he was going to Rock Springs. "So you have an older brother and sister?"

"Yes. My older sister was named Lucy, but when she was fifteen, she just vanished. No one knows where she went or what became of her, but I am hopeful that Horace might know how to contact her. It would mean a great deal to me to at long last meet her. I understand that she was very strong-willed and independent even as a child growing up with her father and brother at Fort Smith."

"Have you ever met Horace before?"

"Only once that I can remember. He moved out of the house when I was a baby, but he came back to the South one time to do some land business. He seemed nice enough although I was a girl and he paid little attention to me. I just hope he will be hospitable and understanding of my circumstances."

"I'm sure that he will be," Longarm said, doubting it.

"Please understand that I'm not going to Rock Springs to beg for money. I can and will provide for myself, but I have a fine opportunity to buy a business back home that I intend to make very profitable. My brother is a banker and a rancher so I believe he will understand the opportunity and take a fair share for himself in return for his financial investment."

"And if he refuses . . . not that I'm saying it's likely he'd refuse his own sister."

"I come bearing news of an inheritance that will greatly interest him. I have a stake in that inheritance . . . not as large as his own or that of our lost Lucy . . . but a significant stake that has yet to be disbursed."

"I see," Longarm mused. "So your father and family were well to do?"

"Not at all! But I had an uncle named Jim. He was not a nice man but he somehow came into quite a lot of money. Some say he robbed trains and stages . . . even banks. I don't know if that is true or not, but he died quite suddenly in a gunfight just recently."

"And how old was he when he passed?"

"In his early seventies. He was notorious and feared. But he did feel an obligation to his family."

Longarm recalled Lucy telling him how her uncle had raped her when she was little more than a girl. He wondered if Amy had suffered the same fate and decided that she probably had not. "Amy, this is quite a fine story you are telling me."

"I'm only telling it because you said you were a lawman so I know that you are ethical and honest."

Longarm almost smiled. "Well," he said quietly, "you are both naïve and trusting. While most lawmen are honest and brave, some are not entirely without larceny."

"Are you saying there are . . . crooked lawmen?"

"Sure! Just as there are charlatans who pose as clergy

and use the pulpit for their own ambitions and financial gains."

Amy smiled. "Thank you for being so candid."

"You're very welcome."

"And what business brings you to Rock Springs?"

Longarm considered the question carefully and made his decision. "At the moment, I'd rather not say, Amy. But I expect you will find out sooner rather than later."

"How mysterious you are!"

"Amy, you don't even know the half of it," he replied.

Longarm sat with Amy in the dining car for more than an hour. He listened to her tell him about her childhood and even a few things about Lucy. On several occasions he almost confessed that Lucy had been a prostitute who had died after being savagely beaten by two men he meant to find and kill. But each time he had that urge, he stifled it quickly because he wanted to meet Horace Potter and try to figure out if the man had anything to do with Lucy's death. If Potter found out that he was a former United States marshal, Longarm knew that he would get nowhere near the truth.

Best, he thought, *to stay silent.*

At the little rail stop called Table Rock, Amy finally got up to go stretch her legs outside. "I can't tell you how much I've enjoyed our conversation and thank you so much for buying me that delicious breakfast."

"My pleasure."

Amy brushed a strand of light brown hair back. "You really have intrigued me as to your business in Rock Springs."

"I'm sorry that I can't talk about it."

"I understand and it really is none of my business. I am

so excited to meet my brother and go visit a real cattle
ranch."

"Do you plan to stay for long?"

"I've no set time schedule. The business that I hope to
buy is sound and the owners have promised me that they
will not sell to anyone else until I let them know that I've
secured enough funds to buy them out. In fact, they urged
me to enjoy my time in the West and not feel pushed to
make a hasty decision."

"What kind of business is it?"

"Hats," she said. "They make fine hats and sell them
mostly in New York, Boston, Philadelphia, Washington,
D.C., and other big cities. They've been making stylish hats
since the war and have more than two dozen employees.
I've worked for the company as a bookkeeper then accoun-
tant and finally as the financial officer and vice president."

"So you've done rather well."

"I've worked hard . . . especially since my husband was
killed."

Longarm had a question that he could not help but ask.
"Then why are you in such need of money?"

"Oh," she said with a smile. "Yes, that would be confusing. The truth is that I've invested almost all of my wages
except enough to live on into the company. And that is why
I'm now in the position of being short of funds . . . but also
able to actually buy the Hampton Hat Company and take
full control and responsibility for its continued success."

"I see. Maybe someday I'll want to buy one of your
company's hats."

"We specialize in bowlers, but somehow I don't see you
wearing one of those out here."

"You're right about that."

She got up to leave. "I hope we meet again in Rock Springs."

"I'm almost certain that we will."

"Good!"

And with that, Amy Potter turned and walked out of the dining car, leaving Longarm to marvel at how chance so often put him in the right place at the right time. He felt guilty about not being fully forthcoming with Amy and hoped that the day would not come when she would discover that he had been less than forthright in their discussions. But he would take that chance and so he left the dining car a few minutes later and headed to a different coach, where he could think in private while the last fifty miles passed before they reached Rock Springs.

Chapter 12

Longarm lingered on the train while the passengers disembarked at Rock Springs. He watched Amy Dunn as she looked around, anxiously scanning faces. It seemed to Longarm that she might have been expecting someone, but whoever it was did not appear to greet her arrival. Amy finally picked up her bags and started walking into town. Longarm knew that, if she was headed for the bank hoping to find her brother, she was in for a disappointment because it would have already closed for the day.

He picked up his own bag and tipped the porter, who looked familiar but whose name he had forgotten since his last train ride west. "Have a good trip on to Sacramento."

"Thanks, and enjoy your stay in Rock Springs, Marshal."

"I'll try," Longarm replied, not bothering to tell the porter that, for the time being, he was no longer an officer of the law. The man was in his forties, neat in appearance but missing a few upper front teeth.

"Got a long ride across the deserts to Reno," the porter said cheerfully. "That's where my wife and I live."

"Nice town," Longarm remarked as he prepared to step down on the platform. "I've always thought it a beautiful city."

"We like to stroll along the Truckee River and sometimes I'll fish, but the fishing isn't that good. If you really want to catch big trout, you have to go all the way up to Lake Tahoe. The trout there are delicious 'cause they live in such deep, cold, and clear water."

"I'm sure that's true," Longarm said, never much interested in fishing but wanting to seem sociable. "Maybe I'll see you again soon on the eastbound."

"You never know."

Longarm climbed off the train and followed Amy as she made her way into the business district. It wasn't all that impressive, but there were some large stores and shops. Mostly, the businesses here catered to the railroad workers and cowboys, same as they did in Laramie and Cheyenne.

Longarm paused to watch Amy as she came to stand before the bank, which was shuttered and locked. She seemed unsure of where to go or what to do next and he recalled that she was nearly out of funds. Longarm did not want to seem forward but here was a young woman in need of help and he did have all that money that Maggie had given him.

"Mrs. Dunn," he said, approaching. "I see that the bank is closed and you're probably wondering what to do now."

"Yes," she said, looking a bit exasperated. "I was really hoping that Horace or one of his employees would be waiting for me at the train station. I sent a telegram off yesterday from Cheyenne telling my brother that I was arriving."

"Telegrams aren't always reliable," Longarm told the woman. "I'm sure that your brother didn't receive it, or he would have been waiting for you back at the train station."

"He might even be out at his ranch," she said, biting her lower lip. "What am I to do now?"

"Could I offer some assistance?"

"In what way?"

"Well," Longarm said, "I could loan you some funds until you are safely situated."

"Thank you but no. I couldn't ask that of a stranger."

"I didn't think we were strangers anymore," Longarm answered with a smile. "And I really do insist that you accept my offer. After all, what is your alternative for tonight?"

"That's true," she said, not able to hide her apprehension. "In retrospect, I can see that I was counting far too much on my brother, whom I hardly even know. He might not help me and then I'd be in a fine fix. I did at least have the foresight to buy a round-trip ticket back to Charleston, but I'd have to starve on the way home."

She looked so worried that Longarm gently took her arm. "Amy, I've been with you long enough to know that you're a very honest and respectable woman. I insist that you borrow some money and allow me to find you a safe, clean hotel."

"Are there any such places in this rough-looking town?"

"Of course. Just a block up the street is the Rock Springs Hotel, and that's where I always stay. They even have a restaurant on the first floor and the food, while not as good as that on the Union Pacific, is still very good."

"Well . . ."

Longarm removed his wallet. "I think that in order to retain your good name in Rock Springs and not cause undue gossiping, it would be best if I just loan you a hundred dollars. Also, I believe we should arrive separately."

"Yes," she said, looking very much relieved, "that would be best. Oh, you're such a gentleman!"

"Not always," he admitted, giving the woman the money. "Go ahead and register and I'll be along a short while later."

"Thank you so much! When I meet with my brother at the bank tomorrow, I'm sure he will give me money to reimburse you."

"Don't concern yourself or worry if you can't repay me promptly," Longarm said, not really caring all that much about the money.

Amy leaned forward and kissed his cheek. "First you buy me breakfast and now you save me from a very difficult situation. You are truly a gentleman of the Old South."

Longarm smiled and walked away. He knew where the sheriff's office was located and he hoped to catch Dub Turner before the man locked up for the night . . . if he slept elsewhere. Many of these small railroad towns had a sleeping room attached to the sheriff's office so that they could pay the lawman a lower salary.

"Well, well!" Sheriff Turner exclaimed, dropping a cleaning rag and laying down his pistol on his desk. "As I live and breathe, it's none other than the famous Longarm. What brings you to Rock Springs?"

Longarm shook the man's hand and took a seat. "I had a while to spend in Cheyenne, and Sheriff Gibson told me that you'd left him to become the sheriff here. Congratulations, Dub."

"It was hard to leave Cheyenne. I worked for Gibson for five years, and he taught me all that I know about being a railroad town sheriff. More than once he bailed me out of some bad situations and even saved my life a time or two. When I started to work for him, I thought that I was tough and capable enough to handle any situation, but I soon learned differently."

"I'm glad you appreciated the apprenticeship and learned from it. A lot of young men like yourself have been killed because they never had a mentor and were forced into deadly situations that they were not prepared to handle."

"I'm sure that's true," Dub said. "I'll put on a pot of coffee if you want."

"No thank you. I just stopped by to pass along Sheriff Gibson's best wishes and to see how you're getting along."

Dub shook his head. "It's quite a bit smaller than Cheyenne, but the politics are pretty much the same."

"And how is that?"

"Well," Dub began, "what I've come to understand is that all these little railroad towns are political as hell. There are a few men who often don't even hold an official office but have the money and therefore the power to make the important decisions and call the shots. They finance the election campaigns and ensure that the men that do get elected are their favorites."

"Yes, that's often true even in the bigger cities. Money is power."

"It sure is," Dub solemnly agreed.

"Were you backed by the power interests here in Rock Springs?" Longarm bluntly inquired.

"I'd like to tell you no . . . but that wouldn't be entirely the truth. There are a few wealthy people here that I'm beholden to . . . but I'd never do their bidding if it was in the wrong, unfair, or illegal."

"Glad to hear that."

"I miss George Gibson a lot," Dub confessed. "He was like a father to me. We talked all the time about the law, and George could tell stories for hours about all the characters . . . good and bad . . . that he'd met during his long years of being a sheriff. I greatly admired the man."

"He is one of the best," Longarm agreed. "So have you had a smooth start here in Rock Springs?"

"Oh," Dub said, frowning, "I'm not sure if 'smooth' is how I'd describe it. I've had some battles . . . both in bar rooms and in the back rooms. I'm earning my money . . . that's for sure. I eat and sleep in that tiny room behind the back door that isn't as big as my jail cell. It was so dirty and flea infested when I moved in that I was scratching like a hound for the first week and covered with bites. I had to boil water and scrub it down twice. Change the mattress and all the bedding. The man that was sheriff here before me was slovenly."

"Well," Longarm said, not sure what to add to that line of conversation, "hopefully he was at least honest."

"I don't know," Dub said, "because he was shot dead before I arrived. Some say he started visiting the Chinese and developed a great fondness for opium. That he got deep in debt and was killed because he refused to pay."

"Then you've got an easy act here to follow, Dub."

"The railroad workers hate the cowboys, who hate them back even more," Dub said. "Not that much different than up in Cheyenne except that Sheriff Gibson made the rules strict enough that both sides toed the mark because they knew that he would come down hard on them and he was backed by a tough, hanging judge."

"What's the judge like here?"

"He's a farce!" Dub said angrily. "He owns a saloon that

isn't doing well and takes the bench whenever he is told to or can make a few extra dollars. I've already seen him hand down some damned questionable sentences. Some fellas get off scot-free when they would have faced a lot of jail time in Cheyenne . . . others seem to be punished way beyond their crimes. I don't understand it, but I've been told that what the judge does is none of my business."

"But it *has* to be," Longarm countered. "Without a strong but fair judge on the bench, your authority and respect as sheriff of this town are greatly weakened."

"I know that and I mean to see if I can get the current judge replaced as soon as possible. But for now and being new . . . well, I figure that I had just better keep my head down and my mouth shut or I might get fired."

"Sheriff Gibson told me to tell you that you have a job back in Cheyenne if you need it."

"That's real decent of him, Marshal."

"What can you tell me about Horace Potter?"

"Why do you ask?"

Longarm shrugged. "I have my reasons."

"I'm sheriff now and I think I deserve to hear them," Dub said. "You're asking about the most powerful man in this town and county. Has he done anything illegal?"

"I don't know," Longarm replied. "But it's a long and complicated story that I haven't the time to tell you right now."

"I won't sleep tonight if you don't at least sketch it out for me, Custis."

"Okay. You should know that I'm here primarily to arrest or kill two men who murdered a girl in Denver named Lucy Potter."

Dub's eyebrows lifted. "I take it that she must be some relative of Mr. Potter's?"

"Horace Potter is her older brother."

"So what has he got to do with his younger sister's death?"

"I'm not sure," Longarm confessed. "Lucy Potter was a prostitute that had some inheritance coming from the Potter estate back in Charleston, Arkansas. I don't know the details and they really aren't important. The point is that Lucy was murdered by a couple of hard cases named Willie Benton and Pete Rafter. Lucy died in my arms after telling me that they were the ones who had beaten her so badly."

"Wait a minute!" Dub said, throwing up his hands. "I'm not following this. What has this woman's death to do with Horace Potter?"

"Maybe nothing, Dub. But there is the chance that the pair was hired by your Mr. Potter to kill Lucy so that he would get more of the inheritance."

"That doesn't make any sense at all," Dub scoffed. "Mr. Potter owns our bank and has a big ranch. He doesn't need any inheritance!"

"You can never be sure," Longarm argued. "I've known plenty of rich and influential people who have gotten into high finances and big trouble."

"I don't believe this."

"Look," Longarm said. "I intend to meet Mr. Potter and just see if I can get a feeling about the man. But what I'm really hoping is that Pete and Willie show up here to either get paid by the banker . . . or try to extort some money from him."

"You're fishing without any bait on your hook, Custis. Horace Potter has a bad reputation for swindling small people out of money. He'd tell you that he's as honest as the day is long, but I'd tell you I've heard stories about his business practices that prove otherwise."

"If he will swindle people out of their property and money, then he might also be willing to hire murderers to increase his inheritance."

"I'm not buying into that one."

"Doesn't matter to me if you do or not, Dub. Pete and Willie vanished from Denver and I've no idea where or how to find them. For all I know, they might be headed for New York City or New Orleans. But this is my best chance to catch them and that's why I'm here."

"I can't help you with Mr. Potter. I owe my job to the man."

"I figured that out already," Longarm said. "All I'm asking you is to just let me hang around for a while and see what turns up. If the pair of killers don't arrive in a week or so, I'll have to rethink everything."

Sheriff Turner was clearly upset. "Look, Custis, I know you are damn near legendary as a lawman, but I can't let you go snooping around and bothering the most important citizen of Rock Springs."

"I won't bother the man."

"Sure you will! How do you think he's going to feel when a United States marshal shows up at his bank or ranch and starts asking him about the murderers of his sister?"

"I don't know or care." Longarm could see that further conversation was going to only upset the young sheriff even more so he rose to his feet and said, "We'll talk more soon."

"If you're going to do what you said, I'd as soon you got on the eastbound train tomorrow and went back to Denver."

"Can't do that, Dub. I have to find those two killers." He described both men and their stolen horses. "Appreciate it if you'd keep your eye out for them," he said on his way out.

"Where are you staying?"

"The Rock Springs Hotel."

"Maybe we ought to have dinner together now and sort this out better."

"I'd prefer that we just keep some space between us, Dub. Be better for you and me."

"I don't like this at all."

"I promise what I do here will not cost you your job."

"It had damn well better not!"

"Have a nice evening. Oh, one other thing. A lady by the name of Amy Potter arrived with me on the train."

"Another Potter mystery woman?" Dub asked with disbelief.

"Yeah. But she's come to inform Horace about the inheritance and ask for a loan."

Sheriff Dub Turner shook his head. "This is more tangled than a can of worms."

"You must like to fish," Longarm remarked as he closed the door behind him.

Chapter 13

Ten miles west of Laramie, Pete Rafter staggered into the railroad town of Bad Water feeling more dead than alive. He was so exhausted, he could barely move, and his feet had swelled up so much in his boots that he was sure he would never be able to walk much anymore. The street was about fifteen one-story buildings long on each side with the usual sad collection of whorehouses, saloons, and a few dry goods stores. There were some houses, a gunsmith shop, and he could hear the ring of a blacksmith's anvil. No churches or schools, of course, but there was a railroad yard and repair shed next to a water tower and a mountain of coal. And at the west end there was a livery stable beside a telegraph office. He couldn't see anything that might be a jail, which wasn't surprising because this town looked like it had long since seen its best days.

I got to have food and drink, Pete said to himself. *But where do I get the money? The way I look, nobody is likely to help or hire me so I gotta steal what I need.*

Pete had been a thief and a pickpocket his entire life. He'd been rolling drunks since he was a teenager and had no problem with his conscience. Some men were lucky and had a lot . . . some were unlucky from birth and had to take from those who had more . . . it seemed simple and right somehow.

He inspected his pockets, knowing he would find nothing of value. He was so hungry and tired from walking into the cold Wyoming north wind that he was still chilled to the bone. At the first store he passed, people stared at him through the window, and when he saw his gaunt, bedraggled reflection, he understood why.

Pete stopped in front of the first saloon he came to and he swore he could smell the pickled pigs' feet and sausages given freely to the regular paying customers. He squared his shoulders, lifted his chin, and pushed his way inside, surprised to see the saloon was smoke-filled and crowded. The beer and whiskey flowed, and men were laughing and talking like they hadn't a care in the world.

"Excuse me," Pete said, sidling up to a short cowboy with a fine Stetson hat leaning against the bar, which was nothing but a couple of rough planks resting on empty beer barrels, "but I'm broke and I sure could use a drink. Would you show a little Christian charity to a man whose luck has turned real sour?"

The cowboy stared at him for a minute, and he was tilting back and forth so Pete figured he was already drunk.

"Well now, that depends," the cowboy said. He was cross-eyed, and Pete wondered if it was due to the whiskey or if he'd been born that way. "You lookin' for a handout or a job?" He tossed down his drink and belched.

"Either one," Pete replied. "Misfortune has been my calling card as of late and I just need a little help."

"Well, gawdamn," the cowboy exclaimed, belching again, "how'd you come upon such bad luck?"

"I was wronged by a mean and evil Jezebel woman," Pete said, the lie coming quick and easy. "Two months ago I was a man of some respect in . . . in Omaha, Nebraska. I owned a nice little house and . . . and a livery stable. Then I met Miss Gertie and she stole my heart."

"Was she a lady by reputation . . . or just a wormy whore?"

Pete sighed as if he were the saddest and biggest fool who ever lived. "She was a whore but I thought I could make her an honest woman by marrying her. She wound up stealing every dollar I'd saved and then hiring a slick lawyer who forged some papers givin' her my house and all my worldly possessions."

The cowboy rocked back on his boot heels and nearly went over backward. His friends saved and got him straightened up. "You married a *whore*?"

"I know I was wrong, but . . . but she had a good story. That woman lied me plumb into the poorhouse."

"By gawd," the cowboy gasped, "what kind of fools live in Nebraska? That's hard to believe they all skinned you clean."

Pete held his hand up to his heart. "I swear to God it's the truth, or may I burn in hell forever. Gertie probably paid the sheriff and the judge part of what she stole from me . . . and it was considerable. I was busted, jailed for a month, and then run out of town. I been trying to make my way west ever since doin' odd jobs . . . when I can find 'em. I got a sick mother in Reno."

"Shit, mister, you sure do have a heavy load on yourself."

"I try to be strong and walk a righteous path."

"You don't look very strong right now."

"No, I surely do not."

"Mister," the cowboy said in a low and serious voice, "you *deserve* a drink!"

"Yes, I surely do."

"Hey, Walt!" the cowboy called to the bartender.

"Yeah, Jeb?"

"Two shots."

Even though Pete was sure that one of the shots was meant for Jeb, he grabbed both and threw them down. "Thank you! You sure put a shine back in my life. Now I don't suppose you could slide down there and grab me a few of those pigs' feet and sausages . . . oh, and I see they got some crackers and mustard. I sure would like some of them 'cause I'm awful hungry."

"I ain't no step-and-fetch-it, mister," Jeb said, ordering two more shots and making sure this time he got one of them. "Why don't *you* get yourself something to eat?"

"You think that would be okay?" Pete asked, trying to sound timid and humble.

"Why, of course it would be!" the cowboy bellowed. He turned to a couple of his friends and shouted, "Hey, boys, this here sorry fool married a *whore*!"

Most everyone in the saloon burst out laughing. Pete bowed his head, covered his dirty face, and pretended to cry in shame.

"Aw, Jeb! You done hurt the fool's feelings," someone said loudly. "Poor bastard looks like he's been dragged to hell and back and that he ain't eaten in a month or more."

"Yeah," another said. "Let's help the man out! Boys, how about we pass the hat around and give this stupid sonofabitch a little money to ease his sorrows?"

Pete thought that was the best news he'd heard in a hell of a long time. He kept pretending to cry, hoping that would generate a pile of money. And when the hat was shoved into his chest, he opened his dry eyes and saw that it was full of coins and cash.

"Oh God," he wailed, gazing up at the fly-specked ceiling, "thank you for this milk of pure human kindness. Bestow your blessing on these fine fellas for helping me out here. Jesus said blessed are the poor for they shall inherit the earth . . . well, I don't want to inherit the earth but I sure do need some whiskey and another whore . . . oh, and a big, juicy steak wouldn't hurt me none either, Lord!"

The next thing Pete knew, cowboys and some railroad men were buying him drinks and shoving pickles, pigs' feet, and crackers at him so fast that he damned near choked to death trying to cram them down his throat. And he found that he was belching just like Jeb.

An hour later, Pete was drunk and so full of bar food that he felt he might have to go into the back alley and puke after he shit. But he stayed on until he couldn't hardly eat or drink any more and then he left his newfound friends with a wave and a "Thank you, thank you all, and praise the Lord!"

The cowboys shouted and hooted. Most yelled at him not to marry any more whores but some told him where to find them and which were the best there in Bad Water. Pete staggered out into the cold and headed toward the nearest hotel. No sneaking into a barn and sleeping on straw tonight!

No sir! Suddenly, his whole world had turned sunny and very promising. He wasn't going to have to steal another horse to reach Rock Springs . . . he would buy himself an honest ticket tomorrow and he'd board that train freshly bathed, shaved, and wearing a brand-new shirt.

He stopped and pivoted crazily around on his feet, which didn't even hurt anymore. *Now where was that whorehouse and what was the name of the girl them cowboys said to ask for? Oh, yes, the Red Rooster and her name . . . her name is Hanna.*

Pete shoved the money deep into his pockets. He hadn't counted how much he'd been given and he wouldn't blow it all on the whore either. No, sir, he would just ease his pains and maybe even do a bump or two in memory of poor Willie, who was no doubt being eaten at this very moment by scavengers.

Bless his poor, stupid soul.

Chapter 14

Longarm checked into the Rock Springs Hotel, and as he was starting toward his room, he saw Amy Dunn sitting in the lobby with a magazine. He walked over and said, "I'm going to be eating as soon as I put my travel bag away and clean up a bit. Would you like to join me in about twenty minutes?"

"That would be nice."

Longarm hurried up the stairs, dumped his bag, changed into a fresh shirt, then returned to the lobby to join Amy. "Did you find your room to be satisfactory?"

"Entirely," she said, taking his arm as they entered the dining room, where perhaps a dozen people were eating. Longarm chose a table apart where they could talk privately and they ordered the house specialty, which was pot roast, potatoes, carrots, and biscuits. "But first we'll have a bottle of red wine."

The wine was so good that they ordered a second as they enjoyed their meal. Amy giggled. "I haven't drunk so much wine in a long time. People are watching us, you know."

"I know," Longarm replied, looking around the room. "I wonder if any of them is your brother."

"No," Amy assured him. "I asked the hotel clerk if Horace ate here and he said that he did . . . quite often . . . but that he was out at his ranch at this time of the year because they were doing the big spring roundup. I sure would like to watch that."

"It's usually pretty dusty," Longarm told her. "There's a lot of noise and a roundup is full of action."

Amy leaned closer. "I have a favor to ask."

"Then ask it," Longarm told her.

"Would you rent a buggy and drive me out to my brother's ranch?" Amy fiddled nervously with her napkin and then poured herself more wine. "You know there's a good chance that Horace will tell me to leave. We don't know each other at all."

"I've thought of that, too," Longarm said. "To be honest, your brother has the reputation of being a hard man."

"In what way?"

"In his business dealings," Longarm said without hesitation. "His reputation is for being ruthless and ambitious."

She considered that for a long moment. "I'm sorry to hear that. It doesn't come as a total surprise because our father was a hard man as well. But I do come bearing news of an inheritance to be shared."

"May I ask how much for your brother?" Longarm asked.

"About five thousand . . . same as I get and what Lucy will get if she is ever found alive. The proposition I'm offering my brother is that he invest his inheritance in that hat company I want to buy. That way, he stands to broaden his investments without really losing any money."

Longarm didn't quite understand the logic. If Horace

was due to inherit five thousand, wouldn't he still be losing that money if Amy's hat business failed? Still, he didn't think it worth mentioning his point.

As Amy talked on, they killed the second bottle of red wine. He was troubled over how much he should tell this young woman . . . especially the fact that Lucy was dead.

"Did I say something wrong, Custis?"

"No, not at all," he replied quickly. "But why don't we see what happens tomorrow? If your brother is gracious and you want to stay out at his cattle ranch, well and good. But if not . . . I'll bring you back to town."

"And then I'll just have to board the eastbound train and return to Arkansas," she said, shrugging her shoulders. "In time Horace will receive his share of the inheritance and so will I. An equal amount will be distributed to the other inheritors, and I suppose Lucy's share will be held in a trust until she is found dead or alive."

"That sounds about right," Longarm said, ordering a brandy instead of a dessert.

"I think I'd like a brandy, too," Amy said.

When the drinks came, they toasted. "Amy, here's to a successful meeting with your long-lost brother, Horace."

"And to a successful meeting with whoever you came to Rock Springs to meet," Amy offered.

In the upstairs hallway next to their respective rooms, Longarm almost told Amy about her dead sister. Also, that he was in Rock Springs looking for Lucy's killers and perhaps even a link between them and Horace Potter. But again, something told him it was better to remain silent at least until he had a chance to see Horace tomorrow at the roundup.

"Custis?" she whispered, "I have a feeling that you

haven't told me something very important that I should know."

Longarm said nothing.

"Why don't you and I talk awhile longer," she said, unlocking her hotel room door. "I think that we need to share our . . . our intimacies before we ride out to the ranch."

"All right."

Amy's room was identical to his own, and both overlooked the town's main street. Longarm went to the window and opened it, needing some cold to sharpen his wits. There were quite a few men down on the boardwalks laughing, talking, smoking, and drinking. At least twenty horses stood dozing at the hitching rails, and two different pianos were playing although one was badly out of tune.

Longarm stared out the window for several minutes, and when he turned around, he blinked with surprise. "That was sure fast!"

Amy was standing by her bed. She had a lovely body and she wore nothing but a smile. "There's a chance we might not meet after going to the ranch tomorrow, and I wanted to remember you in all the important ways."

"Like making love?"

"Yes. I never in my wildest dreams thought that I'd one day be in a Western hotel with a famous lawman. I . . . I haven't had a man since my husband was killed and I thought . . . why not tonight . . . why not with Longarm."

At the name she used, he chuckled. "Who told you that I was known as Longarm and was famous?"

"The porter on the train . . . and a few others I ran into, including a soldier."

"I see. And you didn't say anything until now?"

"No," Amy replied. "I thought you'd like this surprise."

Longarm shook his head. "Well, damned if I don't!"

"Maybe we've talked enough and drunk more than we should have," Amy said, reaching out to him. "I'm convinced we should make love and enjoy what time we have together."

Longarm began to undress. He was already growing stiff. And when he climbed into her bed, Amy's skin felt hot. "I never would have seen this one coming," he admitted.

"Well," she said before kissing him deeply, "for what it's worth, neither did I until you passed on dessert."

"What has that got to do with this?"

"Our desserts are each other," Amy told him as she took his manhood in her hand. "Let's make them special."

As he mounted her, Longarm thought that this was the most special dessert he'd ever enjoyed in Rock Springs.

Chapter 15

"Amy, last night you asked me for the favor of renting this buggy and driving you out here to your brother's ranch," Longarm began after they'd driven a mile out of Rock Springs. "And now, I have a favor to ask you in return."

"Go right ahead."

"I'd like you to keep the fact that I'm a lawman to yourself."

She looked at him curiously. "Do you mind if I ask why?"

"I have my reasons."

Their buggy rolled on for a quarter of a mile before she asked, "Is there someone employed by my brother you intend to arrest?"

"Perhaps," Longarm said.

"Someone who has done something terrible?"

"I'm afraid so."

"What do I say when Horace asks who you are and what my relationship is with you?"

"I've been giving that some thought," Longarm told her.

"Why don't you just say that I'm someone that you . . . you intend to marry."

"What?" Amy's mouth dropped open. "Are you serious?"

"Of course not. You dream of buying a hat factory in Arkansas, and I have no interest in leaving Denver."

Amy thought a few minutes as they rolled along. "This is all about that something important that you're not telling me, isn't it?"

"It is."

Amy reached over and grabbed the lines, pulling their horse to a stop. "I don't want to go any farther until we're completely honest with each other. I believe that after what happened between us last night, we owe it to each other to be candid about matters that affect us both."

Longarm set the brake and hopped down. "Let's go for a short walk," he suggested.

"Only if you'll tell me what is so troubling."

"I'm going to tell you."

He helped Amy down and they walked a short distance to a rise in the land. Far to the north, Longarm could see a big cloud of dust and the faint outlines of buildings and trees. "That's probably your brother's ranch and the dust cloud is where they're working the cattle they've rounded up and driven to the corrals."

"Don't try to change the subject. What's wrong?"

"You said that the last time you saw Lucy, you were five years old."

"That's right. Even though I've seen pictures of her, I'm not even sure I'd recognize my own sister."

"And that Lucy had always been wild."

"Very wild. But . . ."

Longarm couldn't see any way to soften the blow that

he was about to deliver. "Amy, I was with your sister when she died not long ago in Denver. She'd been beaten to death by two men, and I'm bound and determined to find them and kill them on sight."

Amy took a sharp intake of breath. "Custis, why didn't you tell me this sooner?"

"I wanted to, but I just couldn't. You see, Lucy knew about the inheritance. I don't know how . . . but she did. And when the two men killed her, I think they *might* have been working for your brother."

"Doing what?"

"Making sure that Horace's slice of the inheritance was larger."

"That's crazy!"

"It might be," Longarm admitted. "But I've been a lawman for a lot of years and I've learned to listen to my hunches. If the men that murdered your sister show up in Rock Springs and go straight to your brother, then it tells me one of two things. Either they don't know Horace but are going to try and extort some big money out of him . . . or they were hired by him to kill your sister."

Amy shook her head as if she needed to clear her vision. Finally, she said, "I . . . I don't understand any of this, Custis. How on earth could they extort money out of Horace?"

"Rock Springs is a small town. In small towns out in this country, everyone pretty much knows everyone's business. Few secrets can be kept, and the one secret that would have greatly harmed your brother was the fact that Lucy was a prostitute."

"No!"

"It's true," Longarm said with sincere regret. "I was trying to help Lucy out when she was murdered. And while it might have just been a coincidence or had nothing to do with her forthcoming inheritance, that's something I have to learn the truth about."

"My God," Amy said. "I can't believe what I've just heard. My sister was a prostitute that was murdered and you think my successful brother might have actually hired her assassins?"

"I'm afraid that's about the size of it." Longarm lifted her chin and looked into her eyes wet with tears. "Amy, despite her profession, your sister was a good person. Out in the West, women have very few choices, and often they boil down to being married and respectable, or unmarried and trying to survive by plying the oldest profession."

"How very sad."

"Yes," Longarm agreed, "it is. But that's the way of it and Lucy made her choice many years ago."

"Were you—"

"No," Longarm said quickly. "I never made love to your sister."

"Thank heavens for that much, at least."

"But I cared about her very much, and I mean to find her killers. I think they are coming to Rock Springs, and I have to know if they were hired by your brother."

Amy looked off into the distance, but she wasn't seeing anything, just feeling. "How are you going to ask my brother about his involvement in our sister's murder?"

"I don't know," Longarm confessed. "I've been thinking about it since I left Denver. Maybe I won't ask him. Maybe I'll just watch and listen and try to figure out the truth."

"What am I supposed to do?"

"Don't tell him who I am or what I came to learn," Longarm said. He took Amy's hand and they started back toward the buggy. "Maybe your brother will ask me to stay at the ranch with you, but I'm not counting on it. I'll just fish for whatever information I can get. Most importantly, I won't give him any indication that I've come to see if he's behind his own sister's death."

"If my brother even suspects—"

"He won't," Longarm said quickly. "Not unless you give him my true reason for meeting him."

"Custis, is this the *real* reason you've helped me? Is that what's behind your kindness?"

"No," Longarm said, taking her into his arms. "It's because I felt close to you from the minute we met. Oh sure, I knew you were looking for Lucy . . . but I would have had that attraction even if she had never existed."

"I almost wish she hadn't," Amy said quietly before they shared a tender kiss.

The ranch house was huge, and its walls were built of stone and mortar like a lot of the old Indian trading posts. It had a spacious front porch and a lot of windows. There were several hitching rails, and two big cottonwood trees shaded the west end, where more chairs were placed around a wooden table that probably saw a lot of use on hot summer days. The barns and corrals were equally impressive, and overall the ranch had the feel of substance and lots of money.

Longarm drove the buggy over to the house and helped Amy down. They tied the horse to a hitching rail and started walking across the yard toward the corrals, where cowboys were working the cattle. Longarm could smell the burned hair and flesh and knew that they were branding the calves and most likely cutting off testicles. There were dogs everywhere, and a rooster stood crowing on a fence post some distance from the commotion.

One man was dressed quite differently from the others. He was tall, thirty pounds overweight, red-faced, and perched on the top rail of a fence overseeing the proceedings. Now and then he would shout and point and the cowboys would do his bidding.

"That's got to be your brother, Horace," Longarm said.

"Yes, that's Horace all right. He looks to have put on some weight since I last saw him."

"We shouldn't interfere right now. Why don't we skirt around the corrals and find a place where we can observe? If your brother minds our being here, he'll let us know soon enough."

"I'm sure he will," Amy said.

Longarm and Amy found a good place to watch the cowboys work the cattle. They were efficient and each man in the big corral had his special role. The most interesting cowboys to watch were the ropers who charged in and out of the milling herd of cows catching the calves. The dust was thick enough to cut with a knife, but the ropers seemed to know exactly which animals they needed. Once their loop settled over a calf, they spun their pony around and dragged the bawling calf to some men who tended a fire with several branding irons hot enough to glow red. A cowboy would grab the calf, throw it to the ground, yank the rope off its neck, and at the same time two other men would charge forward . . . one to hold the calf still and the other to jam the branding iron into the hide and hair. At that moment the calf would bawl and thrash but it was helplessly pinned to the dirt with a cowboy's knee to its neck.

"This is pretty brutal," Amy said.

"It's necessary work. If you feel faint from the sight or smell, you should go sit on the porch."

"I'm not going anywhere yet," Amy said. "And by the way, my brother has been casting glances at us."

"I know," Longarm replied. "I get the feeling he has no idea that you're his sister."

"Not surprising since he would never expect me to come all the way from Arkansas to watch this. It sure is hard on the poor little things," Amy said to Longarm loud enough to be heard over all the noise and the bawling of the calves and their mothers.

"You haven't seen the half of it," Longarm told her as a cowboy rushed in and, with a quick stroke of his knife, cut off the calf's testicles then hurled them over to the dogs who were slavering in wait and devoured the bloody little bags in an instant.

Amy looked a little faint as the branded, castrated calf, who was still bawling its head off, jumped up and wobbled back into the herd to rejoin its mother.

"Not pretty, I know," Longarm said, "but that's the way it's done. Sometimes they also notch the ears so they can see the marking easier out on the range, but these cowboys aren't bothering with that today."

"It's a wonder the little ones survive such treatment."

"They look weak, but they're mighty tough," Longarm told her. "No rancher is going to do things that will kill his livestock and eventual profits."

They watched the cowboys for almost an hour until Amy walked away. Longarm followed her back to the ranch house, where they each took a rocking chair.

Another hour passed, and from what could be seen and heard, the branding and castrating of calves did not slow down.

"It's nearing noon," Longarm said after consulting his

pocket watch. "They'll soon be stopping to eat and take a rest. I expect your brother will be coming to ask about us before much longer."

"I doubt he'll even recognize me," Amy said. "This ranch is big and impressive, isn't it?"

"Yes, it is," Longarm said. "I have no idea how much land your brother owns, but it must be a considerable amount of acreage."

"I wonder what he's like and what he'll say when he finds out I'm his sister and you are my . . . my betrothed."

"It will be interesting, Amy. I'm every bit as curious as you are."

"I'm sure." She reached out and squeezed his hand. "If you come to suspect that my brother had anything to do with Lucy's murder, please don't let me know when we are all together because I won't be able to hide my feelings."

"I won't say a word or give you any idea. Even if I knew for certain that Horace hired the pair of killers, I'd be an idiot to say something here at his ranch."

"You'd confront him in town."

"Of course," Longarm said. "If there is anything I've learned over the years, it's that a good lawman chooses the time and the place where he intends to make an arrest."

"I don't think that there is a snowball's chance in hell that my brother had anything to do with Lucy's death."

"In one way, I hope you're right," Longarm said just as Horace Potter emerged from the dust to come walking toward them with a look on his face that was anything but friendly.

Chapter 16

"Good afternoon!" Longarm said as the tall man grew near. "You have quite a crew working all those cows and calves."

"Who are you and what are you two doing here?" Horace Potter demanded. "I'm sure I haven't met either of you before, and I'm too busy to have my time wasted."

"You've met *me* before," Amy said. "I'm Amy, your youngest sister from Charleston, Arkansas."

Potter was caught off guard and, for a moment, was speechless. But he recovered quickly. "And who is this with you?"

"My name is Custis Long. I'm Amy's friend."

Potter glared at Longarm and finally said, "I'm sure that I should seem happy to meet you both . . . but you come uninvited and at a very bad time. The roundup is nearly completed, and as you saw, we're very busy right now."

"I'm sorry for the poor timing," Longarm said, trying to curb his rising anger at this insensitive, self-important man, "but your sister has come a long way to meet with you, and she sent you a telegram announcing her arrival yesterday on the train."

Potter shook his head. "If she did, I didn't get it. But even if I had gotten your telegram, Amy, I would have ignored it. I'm just too busy to be bothered with whatever it is that brought you to my ranch."

"Too busy," Amy said quietly, "even to hear about an inheritance due you?"

Longarm had been waiting for this question and the reaction it brought from Horace Potter. He was sadly disappointed that there was no reaction at all from the wealthy rancher and banker. Just a blink of the eyes, then a shake of the head.

"You say that you came here because I'm due an inheritance?"

"That's right. As I am."

"And . . . if I may be so blunt, what is the amount? A hundred dollars perhaps . . . or five hundred . . . although I doubt that our father or our entire worthless Arkansas family had that much money between them."

Amy's cheeks flamed and she was quiet for several moments. "I think," she was finally able to say, "that coming all the way out here has been a huge mistake and that I'll leave now with Custis and you can learn about the inheritance some other way . . . possibly."

Horace Potter removed his expensive Stetson to reveal that he was almost bald even though Longarm didn't think he'd yet reached the age of forty-five. The crown of his head glistened with sweat, and he pulled a monogrammed silk handkerchief from his back pocket and patted his perspiring dome.

"Perhaps I've been a little hasty," Potter offered. "I've

been awake since long before dawn, and we've been working hard to get this task finished during the next few days. The cows and calves are under a lot of stress just like my ranch hands. I owe you an apology."

"Thank you," Amy told her brother.

"I would invite you into my home but . . . well, things are a little chaotic right now and—"

"Who are these nice visitors, Horace?"

They all turned to see a girl who could not have been more than seventeen standing in the doorway. She was wearing a pink housedress, and her hair was pulled back and tied with a white bow. She was extraordinarily beautiful with shoulder-length black hair, luminous dark eyes, and a flawless complexion. Her voice carried an accent but it was not one that Longarm could identify. He judged her to be either Mexican or perhaps one of the Indian peoples of the northern plains country . . . perhaps Sioux or Cheyenne. She wore sandals and her toenails were painted red like her long fingernails. The girl was so stunning that Longarm took an involuntary breath and had to force himself not to stare.

"Maria, it's none of your concern. Please go back to whatever you were doing and allow me to speak in private to these people."

"Are they staying for lunch?" she asked, giving Longarm in particular a warm smile. "If so, then I'll fix—"

"They're *not* staying," Potter said snappishly. "They have to go right back to town."

"Well," Longarm said, giving the girl his most engaging smile. "We're not really in all that much of a hurry. I would like a glass of cool water."

"I would be pleased to make you some lemonade," Maria offered. "And you, miss?"

"Lemonade would be very much appreciated," Amy told her.

"I will bring it out soon along with some sandwiches and cold slices of apple. It is so dusty out there and I saw you watching the cowboys at work. Aren't they very good at what they do?"

"They are," Amy said, extending her hand. "I'm Amy and this is my friend and traveling companion, Custis. We're so pleased to meet you."

"I never get to town and so it is a great pleasure to meet our rare visitors."

"Maria," Potter ordered, "please go back inside."

"I'll return with the lemonade and other refreshments."

The moment she was gone, Longarm exchanged glances with Amy and her look reflected their mutual confusion.

"Your wife?" Longarm asked.

"Of course not! Maria Valdez is my housekeeper and cook. Maria's father worked for me briefly. José was a fine man, but was killed in an accident. She has a brother named Rico, but he is a bad one and the last I heard he was serving time in prison."

"In Cheyenne?"

"I believe in Lincoln, Nebraska."

"For what?"

"Horse theft and assault. It's all very upsetting to Maria and I would ask you not to mention any of this when she returns. When she gets overly upset or excited, she has serious problems."

"What kind, if I may ask?" Amy was frowning.

"Well, it's rather a delicate subject," Potter told her as he lowered his voice in confidence. "But you are my sister so

I'll tell you and know that you'll not say anything about Maria to anyone."

"Of course not."

"When she gets excited," Potter began, choosing his words with care, "Maria loses control of her emotions and her . . . well, her bodily functions."

"Oh my God!" Amy said quietly. "I'm so sorry! Has she seen a doctor?"

"Of course. But there seems to be no help for her. The doctor said that, in time, she might outgrow the problems, but there are no assurances that will ever happen. That's why I keep her away from town. I know you'll both understand and say nothing."

"Of course not," Longarm said.

"And Maria's mother?" Amy asked. "What—"

"Lakota Sioux. She also died long ago of chickenpox. Maria doesn't even remember her."

Longarm couldn't resist. "And have you been together for long?"

"If you mean has she worked for me for a good while, the answer is yes. Maria has nowhere else to go, and this ranch and my house have been her home since she left the orphanage many years ago. She was taught by the nuns up in White Cloud, South Dakota, and when she was eleven, I permitted her father to bring the girl down to our ranch so that they could be together. They were very close, and as you can imagine, when José died, she was grief-stricken. I had no choice but to offer her lifetime employment."

"Is the girl educated?" Amy asked.

"Oh, yes! Maria is a very bright girl and a fine student. When I'm here at the ranch, we read and study together."

Longarm cleared his throat. "Study *what*?"

"History. Great literature. Poetry and philosophy. The girl is like a sponge and has read every volume in my library."

"How very kind of you to take her in and provide for her," Amy said without a hint of sarcasm. "And will she be leaving someday?"

"Only if she wishes and can stand the strain." Horace removed his hat again and wiped his crown.

"She must be the apple of everyone's eye on this place," Longarm said. "Maria is very beautiful."

"Yes, and that has caused some problems. I . . . I try to protect her but some of the younger men find her irresistible."

"I can easily believe that," Longarm replied.

Horace Potter blushed and it was clear that Maria was a source of both great enjoyment but also embarrassment to the man. Longarm had trouble not smiling at the wealthy man's obvious discomfort. For someone of his position, to keep a girl like Maria virtually a hostage would cause tongues to wag in Rock Springs. Therefore, Longarm was quite certain that few people outside this ranch even knew of the girl, who likely was Potter's young mistress. If Sheriff Dub Turner knew about Maria, he would have mentioned the fact. But then again, maybe Maria was someone that everyone here knew better than to talk about.

"You'll excuse me while I wash up," Horace said. "Please make yourself comfortable. It's a fine day and you seemed to be enjoying the porch when I arrived."

"We were," Longarm said as the rancher hurried inside.

They returned to their rocking chairs and rocked quietly for several minutes before Amy whispered, "What do you think?"

"About?"

"The girl!"

"I'd like to withhold judgment."

"My brother could be telling the truth about her."

"Amy, there *isn't* a prison in Lincoln, Nebraska, and there never has been. I'll find out what else your brother is lying about, trust me."

"So do you think that it's *all* a lie?"

"Most really good liars blend truth with their lies so that it sounds better. Maria's mother and father might well have been who he told us they were. Right now, however, I'm more interested in finding out if he had anything to do with your sister's death in Denver."

"I just can't believe that Horace would have anything to do with that."

"We'll see," Longarm told her.

Thirty minutes passed as they sat together on the front porch, and they both heard angry voices coming from somewhere deep in the ranch house. Finally, Horace Potter appeared with a small tray and three glasses of water. Maria was nowhere to be seen. "Excuse me for taking so long."

"What happened to Maria?"

"She became very excited and had an accident. That made things even worse, and she became dizzy and faint. I ordered her to go to bed for her own sake. I know she'll be sorry not to have been able to join us."

"How sad," Amy said.

"Yes," Longarm agreed as he drank his glass of water. "It is very, very sad."

Chapter 17

Pete Rafter had gotten a quick haircut and shave in the small rail town of Red Desert; he'd also had his new boots shined.

"Welcome back aboard," the porter said with a broad smile as the train's whistle blasted, telling everyone it was about to leave the station. "I see you got a haircut and shave while we took on water."

"Yes, but I didn't have time to eat or shop."

"We'll be in Rock Springs in a few hours. I can recommend a good steak and hotel. There are two large mercantile stores there with reasonable prices. Were you shopping for anything in particular?"

"Not really."

"You'll enjoy Rock Springs far more than you have this town. Would you like my recommendations?"

"Sure," Pete said, continuing to be amazed at how much better he was being treated now that he was well groomed and had a bit of money. "I always like the best."

"There aren't a lot of choices, but the Rock Springs

Hotel is where I'd recommend you dine and stay. It's clean and the food is excellent."

"I appreciate your advice," Pete said, slipping the man a dollar. "That's for being so helpful since I boarded."

"My pleasure and I hope you ride with us again."

"So do I."

Pete found a seat as the train left the station. The land was arid, mostly sagebrush but with some struggling patches of grass. He wondered how many acres Horace Potter owned and how much the man was worth. They had met face to face only once . . . and this next meeting was going to be crucial. Pete knew that, if he played his cards right, he would never have to worry about money again. But if he played them wrong, he was as good as dead.

But my luck has changed for the better, he thought. *Suddenly, in that nothing town of Bad Water, I got a break and I'm never going to be poor or sleep in a stable again. My luck is gold now, but the rich and mighty Mr. Horace Potter is soon to find out that his luck has turned as bitter as alkali.*

Pete gazed out at the vast landscape, and then he closed his eyes and drifted off to sleep. He was awakened later by the porter, who was strolling through the passenger cars announcing that Rock Springs was the next stop and the train would be there for only twenty-five minutes.

It can stay however long it wants, Pete thought as he stretched and yawned, *because this is where I finally get my long overdue reward.*

Rock Springs wasn't much to look at but then most railroad towns weren't. Pete stepped down from the car with his bag and a new derringer in his vest pocket. On his hip he wore a used but very serviceable revolver, set deep in a nicely carved leather holster. He tipped his hat to a lady and headed up the street toward the Rock Springs Hotel with his belly grumbling.

The hotel had a spacious lobby with two expensive chandeliers and a number of fine couches, where gentlemen sat, smoked cigars, and read newspapers or just watched the comings and goings of the guests. Pete registered for a room and the clerk asked how long he'd be a guest.

"Depends on several things," Pete replied, signing the register. "It might be just a day or two, and it might be longer."

"Well, however long you stay as our guest, I hope that you enjoy yourself. Our dining room is open and it is known for its thick beef steaks, breaded lamb chops, and great variety of wines, both American and French."

"I drink whiskey but a steak sounds good."

"Would you like me to hold your bag behind the desk or do you want to go straight up to your room?" the man asked with a big smile. "And a small room deposit is required."

"How much?"

"Five dollars."

"That's fine," Pete said, counting off the money. "I'll take my bags up to my room and come back down to eat."

The man handed him his room key. Pete went up the stairs and found his room, which was small but clean, and it even had a few decent oil paintings on the walls. He left his bag on the bed, admired himself with his haircut and shave, then locked the door and headed downstairs to the dining room.

At the bottom of the stairs, Pete Rafter froze in midstep and took a sharp intake of breath. He gripped the banister to steady himself because, not thirty feet away and

seated at a table eating with a handsome woman, was none
other than United States Federal Marshal Custis Long.

Pete's legs nearly buckled as he whirled around and
headed back up to his room. He walked quickly, but nor-
mally, and when he unlocked his room, he closed the door
behind himself and took several deep breaths.

Longarm is here hunting me!

Pete was so shaken that he had to lie down on the bed
and think. What was he to do now? How could he possibly
go see Mr. Potter and make his demands without being
caught or killed by the federal marshal?

*I have to leave before Longarm sees me. But would he
even recognize me without Willie and with my new suit of
clothes, freshly shaven, and my long hair cut neat and
close?*

Pete stood up and began to pace back and forth.

*Was Longarm here because he saw a connection
between Lucy and her rich Rock Springs brother? And
who was the woman he was sitting at the table enjoying a
meal with? She looked a lot like Lucy. Could she possibly
be the Arkansas sister that Lucy had once spoken about?*

Pete grabbed his bag and left his room with the key on
a table. He would find another hotel and he'd think this
through. He suddenly missed Willie Benton. Willie would
have wanted to ambush the federal marshal and the woman
he was with . . . kill them with shots to their backs, thus
eliminating this unexpected and dangerous complication.

Pete found a fire escape and he used it to get down to the
alley, which was stinking and filled with rotting garbage.
Rats scurried in the looming darkness. Tomorrow someone
at the hotel would probably discover that he had left without notice.

And I signed in with my own name! Stupid!

Pete was sweating and nervous as he exited the alley and hurried down the street. If his name was in the register book and if . . . by some chance . . . tomorrow Longarm found out that he had arrived at the hotel this very night, then he was as good as finished. The famous lawman would not stop until he had hunted him down and gained his revenge.

I must kill the Denver marshal tonight, he decided. *And if that woman is Lucy's sister from Arkansas due some of the Potter inheritance, I'll need to kill her, too.*

Pete's heels beat rapidly on the sidewalk. He was moving fast and plotting even faster about how to murder the pair, and one thought kept bouncing around in his mind.

I can't afford to wait even a day . . . I have to kill them very soon.

Chapter 18

Longarm pushed back his chair and after tossing his napkin on the table said, "It was a fine breakfast but I've got to stop eating so much. What I could really use is a brisk walk right now."

"I could, too," Amy said. "We might get fat if we keep cleaning our plates. But the food here is so good."

"*Too* good," Longarm agreed. "We'll have to make love at least twice a day up in our rooms or we're in big trouble."

"If we make love that often . . . I *will* be in trouble," Amy said, laughing. "Custis, I certainly don't get the impression that you're ready for fatherhood."

"No, I'm definitely not."

"And," Amy whispered even though the dining room was nearly empty except for two couples at the far end of the room, "I sure as hell don't intend to get impregnated by a lawman who will never leave Denver and the Wild West."

"Then we might have to limit ourselves to once a night," Longarm said ruefully.

"I think that would be a wise idea."

He escorted Amy out of the dining room, and they walked up the street, looking in shop windows, nodding a greeting to the people they passed. It was a nice day, a little breezy, but the air was light and bracing.

"This seems like a very friendly town," Amy offered.

"It's friendly because most of the men we've met this morning can't stop staring at you," Longarm replied. "I know they're looking at me with a lot of envy."

"Oh, you say the nicest things."

"It's true," Longarm said. "I'll bet that you're the most beautiful woman in Rock Springs."

"I'm not nearly as beautiful as that girl who lives in my brother's ranch house."

"If not," Longarm said, trying to be diplomatic, "you're a very close second."

"She's a good ten years younger than I am. Tell me, Custis, what are your thoughts on that situation now that we've had at least part of the night to sleep on it? I confess to you that my mind has been going over and over what we saw and heard and I can't seem to come to any conclusions."

"That's because the situation out there is very confusing and unclear," Longarm said as they walked along. "Your brother might be telling the truth, but then there is that business of Maria's brother being in a prison in Lincoln that doesn't ring true."

"He could have simply made a mistake as to the location."

"Yes, he could have. But do you really buy into that story of Maria having a physical problem of controlling her bodily functions?"

Amy shook her head. "Now that is hard to believe."

"And there's that story about her father, José Valdez."

"What about it?"

"Your brother said that José worked for him briefly."

"Yes."

"Well, if the man worked for Horace just a short time . . . why does your brother feel obligated to give Maria lifetime employment?"

"Good question."

"There are a lot of good questions I'd like to ask him," Longarm said. "But as you saw, your brother is pretty close-mouthed about his personal affairs, which is not in itself any indication of guilt. If what he's told us is true, then I can understand his reluctance to go into detail . . . even to a sister."

"What did you think about his reaction to the news of the inheritance?"

Longarm frowned. "To be honest, he seemed pretty skeptical. It's unlikely that the amount would make any difference in his life unless Horace is hiding some big debts that he can't pay and not telling anyone."

"How could he do that in a small town like this?"

"He's the banker," Longarm answered. "A banker would have every motive in the world to keep his finances private."

"Yes, I suppose that's true." She looked up at him. "I really hope that my brother had nothing to do with Lucy's murder. It would almost seem like a double loss to me."

"That's understandable."

They came to the telegraph office near the train depot. Longarm paused, then said, "Wait here a moment while I send off a couple of telegrams."

"To whom?"

"One to Sheriff Gibson in Cheyenne and the other to my boss in Denver. I'm going to find out if they've ever heard of a Rico Valdez . . . and if there is any record of him being in prison either in Wyoming, Nebraska, or Colorado."

"They can do that?"

"Between the two of them, I expect we'll have an answer to that question no later than tomorrow afternoon."

"I'll just window-shop a little while I wait," she told him. "I won't be far."

"And I won't be long," he promised, striding into the telegraph office.

Pete Rafter had been watching them, and he knew that he would never get a better chance to attack than now. The woman was strolling along the boardwalk, and there were only a few people out this morning. Pete decided to use his new double-barreled derringer. It would be less conspicuous than pulling a Colt revolver, and if he moved in close enough to muffle the gunshot, he would be able to step between some buildings and wait for Longarm to emerge from the telegraph office and then he'd shoot the lawman down with his Colt revolver when he raced to the woman's side.

"Afternoon!" Pete said, doffing his new hat as he approached the woman. "Beautiful morning."

Amy barely nodded, giving the man little attention. She had learned long ago to discourage conversations with strange men, and although this one appeared presentable, there was just something about him that set her alarm bells ringing. She certainly didn't want to be rude, but she didn't want to talk to this stranger either.

"Yes, ma'am!" the man continued with a wide grin. "It is a very nice day. Are you new to Rock Springs?"

"I am," Amy said, turning away in an attempt to let him know she was not interested in a conversation.

But the moment she turned, Amy felt the tall stranger push hard up against her and then she heard the loud crack of a gunshot and felt a searing pain in her side. She cried out and pivoted while falling. The stranger fired a second shot, which Amy saw bite into the sidewalk and spit splinters.

The man started to yank his gun from its holster to finish her off, but suddenly and from what seemed like a great distance, she heard Custis shout.

One more shot and then Amy struck the boardwalk and lost consciousness.

Chapter 19

Longarm saw Amy's attacker stagger and grab his left arm while crying out with pain. The assassin dashed away to vanish between some buildings.

"Amy!"

She was bleeding profusely and Longarm knew that she might be mortally wounded. He scooped her up and yelled, "Where's the nearest doctor?"

Several bystanders shouted and pointed back down the street, and Longarm recalled passing a doctor's office only a few minutes earlier. With Amy hanging limply in his arms, Longarm ran down the street and barged into the doctor's office.

"I've got a badly wounded woman!"

A doctor about Longarm's age rushed out from an examining room. Beyond him Longarm saw a patient lying on a table. The doctor took one look at Amy and yelled, "Bring her in there and put her down on the table. George, I've got an emergency here!"

George jumped off the table. "What happened?"

"She was gunned down in the street," Longarm answered. "George, give us some room and privacy."

"Yes, sir!"

When Longarm spun around, the doctor was already using a pair of scissors to cut away Amy's blood-soaked dress so that he could stanch the hemorrhaging.

"On the counter is a jar filled with bandages," the doctor said. "Grab a handful!"

"Here you go, Doc."

The doctor bent close over Amy, pressing the bandages down hard to control the bleeding. "Roll her over onto her side. I need to find out if the bullet passed completely through her body or if it is inside."

Longarm gently eased Amy over, and sure enough, there was a big pool of blood soaking the back of her dress. "It's bad, isn't it, Doc."

"It's not good. But judging from the entry and exit wounds, I think she might have gotten off lucky because the trajectory of the bullet should mean that no vital organs were destroyed."

The doctor took Amy's pulse and then he leaned in and listened to her breathing before he straightened up and started examining her. "I see gunpowder burns on her dress, telling me she was shot at very close range."

"I didn't see how it started. One minute I was coming out of the telegraph office and the next she was being shot. This doesn't make any sense to me."

"Understanding isn't of any importance just now," the doctor said. "I need to get this hemorrhaging under control and keep her from going into shock. If we can accomplish those two things, I think she's got a fighting chance to survive."

Longarm's mind was racing around in circles. Who was the man who had attacked Amy and why? Everything had happened so fast that he had no clear impression of the shooter except that he was tall, clean shaven, and well dressed. Nothing more came to mind, and Longarm was quite sure that his single shot had only slightly wounded the assailant.

Worry and think about the man who shot Amy later.

"All right," the doctor finally said with a sigh of relief. "I think we've almost stopped the hemorrhaging. Her color isn't good but her pulse is still strong and steady."

"Can you really be sure that nothing vital was damaged inside of her?"

"Pretty sure," the doctor replied. "I'll certainly know better after we get her stabilized. But it appears that the bullet missed every organ. I'm going to need you to help me for a while. Have you had any prior experience with wounds?"

"More than I care to remember. I'll do whatever is needed."

"Who is this young woman?"

"Her name is Amy."

"Is she your wife?"

"No. We met on the westbound train and formed an immediate liking and attraction. I helped her out a bit when we arrived and we were just taking a walk after breakfast when someone shot her."

"My name is Dr. Whitfield."

"Custis Long."

"She's a lovely young woman," the doctor said, studying Amy. "I can't even imagine someone like her being attacked in broad daylight. Rock Springs is a tough town, but the men here revere women, and it just doesn't make any sense at all."

"I don't know what to tell you, Doctor."

"Maybe the young woman was here before, and when she returned, an enemy spotted her and acted on impulse."

"Maybe," Longarm said, doubting it.

"She's going to pull through," the doctor said, managing a smile, "but she'll be bedridden for a while. Does she have any family in Rock Springs?"

Longarm thought it better not to mention that she was Horace Potter's sister so he just said, "Amy told me that she's from Arkansas."

"Well, she isn't going home soon, that's for sure."

Two hours later, Longarm stepped out into the bright midday sun and his expression was grim. He and the doctor had gotten Amy transported on a litter over to a home where the doctor said she would receive expert nursing care. He'd given her some pain medicine and Amy hadn't been able to tell Longarm a single thing about her attacker.

But Longarm knew she would tomorrow. Until then, he was going to go back to where she was shot and start questioning anyone who might have seen the shooting.

"Custis!"

Sheriff Dub Turner was running across the street toward Longarm. He slid to a halt and said, "I just heard about the shooting. What happened?"

"Where were you?"

"I had to ride out of town on some business. I just got back to find that everything here has gone to hell in a hand basket. I understand that you were with a woman who was shot."

"That's right."

"Let's go to my office, where we can talk about this."

Longarm paused, considering the request. "All right."

"Do you know who shot her?" Dub asked as they marched toward his office.

"I only caught a glimpse of the shooter. He was tall, well dressed, and clean shaven. Things happened real fast, and I was only able to get off one shot, which probably only nicked him. He ran off and I didn't have time for a second shot."

"If you managed to wound him," Dub said, "that'll make finding him a hell of a lot easier."

"We'll find him anyway."

"Any idea why he'd do such a thing?"

"No idea at all."

"Was the woman that was shot the person you spoke to me about named Amy Potter?"

"Yes."

"The one that came to tell Mr. Potter about a small inheritance."

"It isn't *that* small, Dub. It's five thousand dollars."

"You're right, it isn't small. But to a man like Horace Potter, it isn't that large."

"You never know," Longarm replied. "But if you ask me, Amy Potter, the man who shot her, and Horace Potter must have a connection."

"That's insane!"

"Is it?" Longarm asked, trying to keep his voice from reflecting his anger. "When I find the man that shot her, I'll get us an answer to that riddle."

"Let's get one thing straight right now. You are *not* the law in this town," Dub said, his own voice hardening. "I'm the sheriff and I'll handle this shooting and the investigation."

Longarm had heard more than enough. Sheriff Dub
Turner was a good man . . . or had been when he'd worn a
badge in Cheyenne. But right now he was sounding like
someone who was more interested in protecting his bene-
factor, Horace Potter, than he was in finding out what was
behind Amy's shooting.

"I'll be around," Longarm said, deciding he did not
want to carry on any more talk with Dub, given the bad
feelings that seemed to have sprung up between them.

"Stay away from that ranch and Mr. Potter," Dub warned.
"He has nothing to do with any of this."

"How can you be so sure?"

The sheriff stammered, and before he could think of an
answer, Longarm added, "And before I go, what can you
tell me about that beautiful young girl that is living in Potter's ranch house?"

"You mean Maria?"

"Who else?"

"She's someone he is helping."

"Oh, really?" Longarm challenged. "And what if he is
holding her as a sex slave? She's a *girl*, Dub! Doesn't that
bother you?"

The sheriff's young face flamed with outrage. "Maria
is . . . is damaged! Badly damaged, and if it wasn't for the
kindness of Mr. Potter, she'd be working in some two-bit
whorehouse and probably drugged out of her mind. You
got it all wrong about Mr. Potter."

"If I'm wrong about him and that girl, then I'll apolo-
gize . . . both to you and to Potter. But my gut tells me that
I'm right. What Potter told Amy and me at his ranch yesterday just doesn't add up."

"What are you talking about?"

"How about a young outlaw that we were told is Maria's brother? A kid named Rico Valdez, who is in the prison in Lincoln, Nebraska."

"There isn't a damn prison in Lincoln!"

"I know that," Longarm said on his way to the door. "But that's what your high-and-mighty Mr. Potter told me yesterday. Any idea why?"

"Rico is dead."

Longarm whirled around at the door. "Say that again?"

"I said that Maria's brother is dead. He was gunned down a few months ago back in Cheyenne."

"Are you sure?"

"I'm as sure as anything because I'm the one that killed him."

Longarm was caught off guard. "What the hell happened?"

"He was no good and had just gotten out of prison someplace. He came into our town and started raising hell. I was on duty, and when I braced him, Rico went for his gun. I got to mine first. Ain't nothing else to tell you."

"What did Sheriff Gibson have to say about it?"

"Not much." Dub looked away. "He was never happy when we had to kill a man, but he knew that I wouldn't have done it unless it was absolutely necessary."

"I see."

"Do you?" Dub asked, eyeing him closely.

"Yeah," Longarm said, looking away and for the first time wondering if both he and Sheriff Gibson might have read this young lawman all wrong.

Chapter 20

As soon as darkness fell over Rock Springs, Pete Rafter came out of a hayloft after two days of running and hiding. The shallow wound in his arm ached, but it wasn't too bad. The saloons were filled with boisterous railroad workers, cowboys, and townspeople. A full moon was rising over the sage-covered hills, and the steel rails running east and west gleamed in the moonlight. Throughout the anxious hours of daylight, Pete had been certain that he would be caught and destined for a hangman's noose. He had shot and probably killed a good woman, and the punishment for that crime was sure to be death.

I have to get out of here tonight or they'll find me for sure, Pete thought. *You don't gun down a pretty woman in broad daylight and live to tell about it when you're caught.*

Pete strolled along the boardwalk eyeing the horses tied to the hitching rails. The animals were all thin and hard used, which was the lot of working cow ponies. Pete wished that he still had the paint or the buckskin that he and Willie had stolen from Jonas Reed's Aspen Stables. Those two horses could have easily outrun and outlasted anything tied to these hitching rails that he saw tonight.

For just a moment, Pete thought of Willie lying dead out on the prairie. By now the buzzards and varmints would have picked his bones clean. Pete had his regrets, just like everyone else, but the main one was that he'd killed his companion and left the body to rot on the open ground. Willie had been stupid and dangerous, unpredictable and ruthless . . . yet few better knife fighters had ever lived. He'd been a liability with his broken shoulder and so there hadn't been any choice but to put him down . . . Pete just would have liked to have had the time and the tools to bury Willie properly. Things like that could haunt a man and put a black curse on him.

Pete shook off those dark thoughts as he moved to the end of the street and then walked back, studying the ranch horses very carefully. He would steal the best one and get what was due him from Mr. Potter then he'd leave Wyoming, never to return.

A tall red roan gelding seemed the best animal here tonight. Pete sidled up to the horse, but it eased away, snorting. That was a good sign because it meant the horse still had some fire in his gut. "Easy," Pete crooned, stroking the animal's neck. "Easy there."

The roan calmed down some and Pete checked the cinch and found it loose. Whoever owned this tall red roan thought enough of the horse to make his wait more comfortable. Pete ducked under the roan's neck, hoping to find a rifle and scabbard . . . but there was none nor had he seen a rifle tied to any of the other waiting horses, which was to be expected. A drunken cowboy might be careless and foolish enough to leave a good rifle on his horse waiting for a thief, but a sober cowboy arriving for a few drinks and maybe a tumble with his favorite whore would not.

Pete decided the roan would do just fine. He tightened the cinch and was untying the horse's reins when a voice stopped him cold.

"What the hell are you doing with *my* horse?"

Pete spun around to see a cowboy standing on the boardwalk with his fists clenched. The cowboy looked tough and mad. Pete knew that he could not afford to get into a fight that would draw attention to himself . . . even though he thought he'd probably win.

"Oops," he said, slurring his voice. "You mean this *ain't* my pony?"

"Gawdamn right it ain't!"

Pete cackled and swayed back from the roan. He squinted as if he were trying to kill his double vision. "Well, gawdamn me if you ain't right! This ain't my roan at all!"

The cowboy hissed, "Get away from my roan and go find your own horse, you drunk sonofabitch."

"Sure will," Pete chirped. "I'd have figured it all out the minute I climbed aboard your horse."

"He'd most likely have thrown your drunken ass over the rail and right through the saloon door."

"I expect he would," Pete said. "I just tightened his cinch. Want me to loosen it for you?"

"No. One more drink and I'm leavin' for the ranch. Now git out of here and stay away from these horses."

"I am goin' to do just that," Pete slurred as he tipped his hat. "Sorry about the mistake."

The cowboy offered no response. Pete left and stumbled back to the boardwalk and up the street.

Damn, he thought, *that was way too close for comfort!*

At the west end of Rock Springs, there was a saloon called the Blue Buffalo and it had a painted blue buffalo sign nailed to its front wall. Although the name seemed mighty strange to Pete, he could see that this was a popular hangout for cowboys. Pete knew from watching that day that it also had an upstairs whorehouse.

There were eight ranch horses tied up in front of the Blue Buffalo, and Pete wasn't about to be slow or picky a second time this anxious evening. He passed the horses just once then doubled back after sizing up a decent-looking bay horse tied in the middle of the group. He squeezed in between the dozing horses, found and tightened the cinch, and then untied the animal.

"Back. Back," he ordered in a low voice while pulling gently on the reins and forcing the bay into the street. Pete threw the reins over the animal's neck and climbed into the saddle. The stirrups were at least two inches too short, but he'd suffer them until he was outside town. The bay kept trying to turn to the east, which Pete knew meant that it had come from that direction, but he forced it to head toward where he'd heard Potter's ranch was located.

"Damn you!" Pete hissed. "You ain't goin' home tonight so get that straight in your fool mind!"

The bay threw its head around in anger. Pete wished he had spurs but the leather reins were long and heavy. He whipped the bay hard across the rump and slammed his rounded boot heels into its flanks until it submitted and headed in the right direction. He kept swiveling his head around to see if anyone was following and wondered if they could pick up his tracks in the morning. Most likely not because the road he was following was well traveled and marked by both wagon wheel tracks as well as hoof prints. Unless the cowboy who owned this jug-headed bay knew the pony's tracks very well or it had some kind of special shoes tacked to its hooves, his trail would be impossible to follow.

Man told me the ranch was only a few miles north. I'll be there long before anyone goes to bed. I'll get my money and ride directly south into northeastern Utah, where I'll disappear into big red rock country. Maybe find a Mormon woman in the mountains. Kill her man, bed her, and steal what she has. I'll do just fine once I get far, far away from that federal marshal, Mr. Potter, and that damnable Rock Springs.

An hour later he saw the distant lights of the Potter ranch house and reined in his horse. His heart was pounding and he had to dismount in order to take a piss. Just for a moment he let go of the reins so that he could unbutton his pants and damned if the bay horse didn't bolt and take off at a dead run toward home somewhere to the east.

"You sonofabitch!" Pete yelled, yanking out his pistol in a rage. He almost took aim and shot the bay in the ass but suddenly realized that would give his presence away to the people at the ranch less than a mile off.

He holstered his gun and pulled a cheap cigar from his vest pocket. Rattled and unsure of how to handle the all-important task that lay before him, Pete sat down on a rock and smoked the cigar. When he was finished, the moon was higher and he heard some coyotes howling not far away. The lights in what was probably the bunkhouse went out but the ones in the bigger house remained on.

This isn't going to get easier by waiting around some more, Pete told himself. *Mr. Potter hired you and Willie to find his kid sister and make sure she didn't ruin his reputation as a whore. He didn't say we were supposed to kill her, but after that federal lawman got involved, there just wasn't any choice. When you tell the man about the inheritance, he'll be grateful. He'd better be grateful and he'd better have the cash.*

Pete ground out the stump of his cigar and started walking toward the ranch house. He walked for what seemed like a long time before he came to a fence, and when he crossed into the yard, he was praying that no ranch dogs would set off a ruckus that would bring the cowboys out of their bunkhouse.

I'm going to ask for five thousand, he told himself. Willie and I agreed to take care of the man's whore of a sister for a thousand each, but I'm going to ask for five thousand, and if he ain't willing, I'll pull my gun. Then he'll shit his pants and pay me plenty damned quick. And maybe I'll take whatever I can extra just for all the bother and worry I've been going through since we made our deal in Denver.

Pete stepped lightly onto the front porch. A board creaked loudly and he froze but no one inside seemed to have heard. He eased across the porch to the front door and slowly opened it enough to slip inside.

There was just enough moonlight filtering into the house to show him that it was big and impressive. Pete listened hard for a full minute and then he heard a man cough down a dim hallway. He sure hoped it was Mr. Potter and that the man had been drinking some and was in a good frame of mind. It would be a lot easier if Mr. Potter just paid him off and gave him a good horse and saddle.

Five thousand and not a gawdamn penny less, he vowed. I owe it to myself and to the memory of poor Willie Benton.

Chapter 21

Longarm hadn't slept much that night. Early in the morning, he'd had his breakfast, lingered over a third cup of coffee, then hurried out of the Rock Springs Hotel to visit Amy.

"You look a lot better today than you did last night," Longarm said, taking the young woman's hand in his own. "You really had us worried for a while."

"It all happened so fast," Amy told him as she shook her head in bewilderment. "One second I was standing there looking in a shop window and the very next this man approached. He tried to make some idle conversation and then he shot me!"

Tears formed in her eyes. "Custis, all of my life I've heard and read that the West is a violent place where people get shot all the time . . . but why me? I was civil to the man."

"I don't know the answer to your question. I caught just a glimpse of him before he ducked in between some buildings and got away. You were bleeding pretty badly so I couldn't give chase."

"It . . . it seems so crazy."

Longarm nodded. "There are crazy people out there. Maybe the man was insane or his wife who looked like you jilted him for a lover . . . I just don't know. However, I do need you to give me the very best description you can of him."

She closed her eyes for a moment. "I can see him very plainly. He was tall, well groomed, and nicely dressed."

"Did you see any distinguishing features?"

"Like what?"

"A visible scar?"

"No. But he had a big, crooked nose."

"Which direction?"

She stared at him. "Is it really important?"

"It might be," Longarm told her. "Can you remember?"

Amy closed her eyes again and focused on visualizing her attacker. "Let's see. He was facing me and his nose was bent to . . . to the left."

"Anything else?"

"His eyes were brown and closely set. He was wearing a nice Stetson so I couldn't see his hair color."

"How old would you guess him to be?"

"Early thirties . . . maybe mid-thirties. Certainly not in his twenties or forties."

"All right," Longarm said. "This will help."

"It will?"

"Sure. If I see a man matching that description and wearing a good suit with a nice Stetson, I'll immediately place him as possibly your attacker."

"So what are you going to do next?"

Longarm shrugged his broad shoulders. "In truth, I'm not sure. I am, however, thinking about going back out to your brother's ranch and asking him if he knows of anyone who'd want to kill you."

"I wish you wouldn't leave me. What if that same man came around again to finish the job?"

Longarm knew she had a legitimate concern. "All right," he said, "I'll wait another day and keep looking around town for the shooter. But then I'll have no choice but to go talk to your brother."

"You don't think . . . no! Horace wouldn't ever want to harm me."

"Yes, he is your brother but you don't even know him," Longarm argued. "And don't you think it strange that your sister is murdered by two thugs from Denver that I'm hunting and now someone is so desperate that they try to kill you in broad daylight?"

"I see what you're saying," Amy replied. "Is there any chance that the pair that beat my sister to death . . . I mean . . . is there any chance that one of them is the same man that shot me yesterday?"

"It's impossible to say. Pete Rafter and Willie Benton were very rough looking. They wouldn't likely be well dressed now, and they stole a pair of horses from a Denver stable that would be easy to spot. A paint and a buckskin, and I haven't seen either of those animals here in Rock Springs. And finally, both Pete and Willie were bearded and you said that the man that shot you was clean shaven."

"That's right."

"So I can't see how there is any connection," Longarm told her. "Besides, that pair had been partners in crime for years. Where you'd find one, I'm sure you'd always find the other."

"Then there must not be any connection between the ttempt on my life and the death of my sister."

"It would seem not," Longarm told her. "When I left
Denver on the train, I had hoped that I would come here to
Rock Springs and just wait awhile. In time, Pete and Willie
would come riding in and they'd go out to see your brother."

"And why would they do that?"

"If for no other reason to try to extort some of his money
because they'd taken Lucy out of the picture and increased
his inheritance. But I was all wrong and so here we are with
you badly wounded and I haven't a clue as to where to find
the pair. I'm afraid I've badly misjudged all of this."

She squeezed his hand. "You brought me here and you
took me out to see my brother. You've given me money to
live on while in this town and you saved my life yesterday.
So don't you think that you've done more than your share
of good deeds since leaving Denver?"

He managed a tired smile. "Since you put it that way,
perhaps I have."

Amy squeezed even harder. "So you will stay with me
at least until tomorrow just in case that man tries to kill me
again?"

"I will. It's a promise."

"Thank you!"

Longarm playfully slipped his hand under the covers and
touched her bare thigh. "You can thank me in bed when
you're strong enough."

"You're an absolute devil!"

"I've been called a lot worse," Longarm said as his
hand slipped a little higher on her bare leg.

"What is going on in here?" a stout woman demanded as
she stepped into the room with a tray of food then stopped
to glare at Longarm.

"Nothing, I'm afraid," he told her as he got out of her way.

"You ought to be ashamed of yourself, sir! This poor young woman almost *died* yesterday!"

"I know."

"And still you're trying to do your funny business under her bedcovers!"

"I really am a devil," Longarm told the woman.

The portly woman studied him closely. "I believe you are . . . but at least you're a handsome one."

Longarm chuckled and so did Amy. He would stay close by Amy's side for another twenty-four hours, but then he really did need to ride out and visit Horace Potter. And this time, without Amy, he would be asking a whole lot more and harder questions of the Wyoming rancher and banker.

Chapter 22

Pete tiptoed down the hallway and decided he ought to be ready for anything. He removed his derringer from his vest pocket and slipped it into his coat pocket, cocked and ready to fire right through the fabric if necessary. He was hoping it would not be necessary. He didn't want Mr. Potter's blood on his hands . . . just his money.

"Mr. Potter?"

The man was sitting at his desk, and when Pete stepped into the spacious, book-lined room, Horace jumped to his feet in surprise. "What are you doing here?"

"We have some unfinished business, sir."

Horace glared at the man. "I told you never to come to me. I said that I'd come to you and Willie."

"I'm a wanted man," Pete explained. "I couldn't stay in Denver and now I can't stay around Rock Springs either. I need to get paid and leave tonight."

Pete waited for an answer, but none was forthcoming.

The tension stretched and Pete's hand tightened on the handle of the deadly little derringer hidden in his coat pocket.

"You need to pay me in cash and I'll want a fast horse. Something to eat from your kitchen stuffed in the saddlebags, a good, straight-shooting rifle, and plenty of ammunition."

Horace's lips tightened into a thin, white line, and he struggled to keep from having a temper outburst. He had never expected to see this man again, but now that Pete Rafter was here, life had become a whole lot more complicated and dangerous.

"Well?" Pete asked, glancing over at a sidebar with crystal decanters. "Aren't you going to offer me a drink?"

"You can help yourself," Horace managed to say. "Then take a seat and tell me the rest of this messed-up story."

Pete filled a crystal glass, and a smug smile never left his now stubbled face. He took a swallow and nodded in approval. "You have excellent taste, sir! It's a taste that I mean to acquire as soon as I've left Wyoming. I'll be taking a couple bottles of this whiskey with me when I leave."

"Tell me everything from the beginning about Lucy and Denver."

Pete nodded and took another swallow. He'd never tasted better whiskey. "Sure, but first I need to know if we're alone in this house or not."

Horace didn't want to tell the man about Maria being upstairs, but even more important, he didn't want to be caught in a lie. Pete was dangerous and unpredictable.

"I have a young woman sleeping upstairs and I don't want her to wake up, come down here, and see you."

"She pretty?"

He ignored the question. "What happened to Lucy? What did you and Willie do to her?"

Pete found a horsehide couch and took his leisure. "Well, now that is a sad, sad story. We . . . we went a little too far."

"You *killed* her?"

"We beat her and she died," Pete said with a shake of his head. "I guess that Willie hit her too hard. I didn't, but he was awful strong and his temper just got the better of him."

"I didn't want her dead!" Horace hissed. "I just wanted her punished and told never to let anyone know she was my sister or to come here and humiliate me. Nothing more."

"Sometimes things don't work out exactly as we want, Mr. Potter. When we learned she was dead, we went on the run. You see, there's this big federal marshal that had taken a shine to her and—"

Horace felt a chill run up and down his spine. "His name?"

"United States Marshal Custis Long."

Potter groaned. "He was here with my sister from Arkansas just a few days ago. Now I know why."

Pete blinked and his smile died. "The Denver marshal showed up here?"

"That's right. I had a feeling that he was here for more of a reason than he was Amy's friend."

"What are we going to do?"

"I'm not going to do anything," Horace told his unwelcome visitor. "I didn't tell you to kill Lucy and I've done nothing wrong. You're the one who has gotten yourself into a mess and face a hangman's noose. And where is Willie?"

"He and I parted company up in northern Colorado."

"If he's caught and talks—"

"He won't be talking to anyone ever again," Pete said quietly.

Horace jumped up and went for a glass of whiskey. He

turned to Pete and said, "You've brought me nothing but grief."

"Pay me off and you'll never see me again, Mr. Potter. I want five thousand dollars right now."

"You're insane!" Horace waved his glass around, spilling his drink. "Do you think I'll pay you that much money for making a total botch of everything?"

"I've earned it. You need to control your temper and pay me enough money so that I'll never come back to Rock Springs with any of this story."

"If you did," Horace said, "you'd be putting a noose around your own damned neck."

"Sure, but you'd be swinging in a noose right beside me. The thing of it is, Mr. Potter, you're rich and I'm dirt poor. We need to help each other out here. Five thousand dollars to you is nothing. To me, it's a new start in life."

Horace Potter knew there was more than a little of the truth in this man's words. And yet he did not trust that Pete would stay away if he was paid off or that he would not be apprehended by the law and then sing like a mockingbird if given promises by the authorities that his testimony would save his worthless life.

Horace knew that there had to be some way to protect himself . . . he just needed a little time to think about it.

"Well," Pete said, draining his glass and smacking is lips. "The night ain't getting any younger. I have needs tonight and you need to see me get a real good start out of Wyoming."

"I don't have that much cash here at the ranch."

"How much?"

"Perhaps only a thousand dollars."

"Hell, I ain't taking that little money! I'm on the run! I need to go far and fast."

"My money is locked up in my bank," Horace said. "I have a vault at the bank so what do you think I do—hide money in a buried coffee can? If you want five thousand dollars, then we'll have to ride into town tomorrow."

"No!" Pete lowered his voice. "I told you that the marshal is in town. He'd see me and I'd be shot on sight."

"Then you'd better take what money I have here along with a horse and get the hell out of Wyoming. It's your choice, Pete, so make it quick."

Pete poured himself another drink and threw it down. "What would your ranch hands say if they saw us leaving at this time of the evening?"

"They know better than to even ask. And besides, it wouldn't be the first time I had to leave suddenly and unexpectedly."

"And you could just get the five thousand and I'll be out of town and on my way by midnight."

"Why not?" Horace asked, trying to sound reasonable. "I want you gone as much as you want to be gone. But if you want five thousand, then we have to go to the bank."

Pete scowled, thinking hard. Finally, he looked up and said, "All right, Mr. Potter. Give me what cash you have here . . . you said around a thousand and I'll take the rest at the bank."

"Deal."

Thirty minutes later, they rode quietly out of the ranch yard and headed to town. The moon was bright, and the air was cool and sweet. The ride would have been a pleasure for Horace if Pete hadn't been beside him, complicating everything that he had ever worked for. It was clear that Pete Rafter was greedy and therefore the man could not be trusted to take the payoff and never be heard from again. That being the case, he would have to die. And what had really become of Willie Benton? Horace was curious, but he was also convinced the man was dead. Most likely he'd been shot committing a petty and stupid crime. Yes, that was what had probably happened to him.

"How is this going to work?" Pete asked as they rode onto the dark main street of Rock Springs. "There are still a few people in the saloons."

"I've been thinking about that."

"I'm sure that you have."

"You stay waiting outside with our horses. I'll go into the bank alone and it won't take five minutes to get the money and return. Then we ride out together and you head south and I'll head north back to the ranch. I'll be in bed by three and Maria won't even have known I'd been gone."

"Is she your mistress?"

"Shut up, Pete. You're about to be another four thousand dollars richer."

"Yeah," Pete said as they dismounted at the hitching rail in front of the bank. "Let's get this over with. The more distance I can put between myself and this part of Wyoming and that marshal, the happier I'll be."

Horace Potter had to unlock two expensive deadbolts to enter the bank. He didn't turn on lights because he knew his way around very well. However, at the vault, he did need a little light to see the combination lock.

He lit a match, spun the dial, and worked it fast. In seconds, he heard the familiar click of the heavy lock mechanism. He snuffed out the light and pulled open the vault's heavy door. All the cash was stacked in piles at the back of the vault, and each banded bundle was a thousand dollars.

Horace grabbed four and turned to leave, only to see Pete standing in front of the vault.

"Lot more cash in there, huh?"

Horace Potter felt a chill run down his spine. "Some."

"Why don't we take it *all*?"

"What?"

"You heard me, Mr. Potter. I want it *all*."

The banker and rancher kept a gun in his desk but that was thirty feet away. He felt his blood turn to ice, and when he spoke, he didn't even recognize his own voice because it was so high and strained sounding. "Please don't do this, Pete. Don't leave me bankrupt and ruined!"

"You've got a big ranch. You'll survive."

"No I won't! I couldn't stand this loss. I *will* be ruined." It wasn't true because the ranch was paid for and the roundup would bring him a sizable infusion of cash, but it sounded good and perhaps . . .

"What a shame," Pete said, lighting a match with his thumbnail. "Well, we all have our problems, Mr. Potter. So grab one of those big money sacks and fill it up. Conversation is over. It's my turn to be rich . . . your turn to be poor. Seems fair to me."

Horace Potter was not a small man and he was not a coward. With a cry of outrage, he lunged across the vault at Pete, who, instead of retreating, charged forward. They met in the middle of the big vault and Pete emptied both barrels of his derringer into the banker's gut at point-blank range.

Horace sagged and dropped to one knee. He looked up at Pete and the flickering light from his match. "Gawdamn you," he squealed. "Damn you to hell!"

Pete stepped back and kicked the rich man in the stomach, where the blood was pumping free. Horace howled

and then he fell over and hit the floor of the heavy vault
with empty, staring eyes.

Pete filled two bags with all the cash he could find. No
doubt there were other stashes in boxes but he didn't want
to spend the time looking. He knew that the steel walk-in
vault had muffled the sounds of his derringer but someone
might be outside wondering why two men were inside the
Rock Springs Bank at such a late hour.

It was time to go . . . and he was rich!

Pete stepped out of the vault just as his match died. He
swung the heavy door shut, spun the combination, and
strode to the front door. He would have locked that one,
too, but realized that Mr. Potter had the outside keys on his
person.

No matter. By the time someone tried the door tomorrow morning, Pete figured he would be twenty or more
miles gone.

*My oh my! I wonder how much cash I have in these two
bags along with the thousand he gave me at the ranch
house. I might be worth ten . . . no, fifty thousand dollars
tonight! My oh my!*

Chapter 23

When Longarm first heard the news about the bank door being left wide open and the vault being locked, he raced out of the hotel and met Sheriff Dub Turner as they were both running across the street. There was a big crowd in the bank and everyone was standing, shouting and angry.

"What's going on here?" Dub yelled.

"The bank's front door was left wide open last night and the vault is locked."

"Then it was probably an oversight," Dub said as they went to inspect the vault.

"Not likely," Longarm told him as he knelt by the floor in front of the vault. He beckoned the sheriff to stoop down close and whispered, "This is the edge of a bloody boot track."

"Oh shit!" Dub gasped. He stood up and looked around. "Who can open this vault?"

A man stepped forward. "The only one who knows the combination is Mr. Potter and he's out at his ranch."

"I'll ride out and get him," Dub offered. "I can have him back here in less than two hours."

"I'll make sure that no one takes anything," Longarm said.

Dub and Longarm ran the crowd outside. Dub sprinted to the stables and it wasn't five minutes later that he was galloping out of town. Longarm stood guard by the front door of the bank because they couldn't get it to lock.

"What do you think happened!" someone in the crowd yelled.

"I don't know," Longarm answered. He could see no good point in telling anyone about the bloody partial boot print. It would only panic the townspeople, most of whom probably had already lost their life's savings.

Although he was no longer an official officer of the law, Longarm appointed two men to act as temporary deputies and gave them orders to keep everyone out of the bank. He hurried over to see Amy and told her what had happened.

"Do you think that my brother robbed his own bank?" she whispered.

Longarm made sure they were not being overheard. "I think this situation is much worse."

"How could *anything* be worse?"

"I believe that Pete Rafter murdered your brother in the vault and took all of the bank's money."

Amy went pale. "No!"

"I can't be certain, but it adds up. If your brother is at the ranch, then we know that we've jumped to the wrong conclusion. The sheriff will be back sometime this morning with the answer."

"I hope Horace is alive and safe."

"So do I."

When Sheriff Dub Turner raced back into Rock Springs, he jumped off his lathered horse and was immediately mobbed by the townspeople. He broke free and jumped up on a horse watering trough and raised his hands. The anxious crowd fell silent.

"Folks!" Dub shouted. "Mr. Potter *wasn't* at his ranch. One of the cowboys saw him and another man leave late last evening and said they were headed south toward town."

People began yelling and talking all at once.

"We need to get that vault opened as soon as possible!" Dub yelled. "Mallory, are you sure no one else knows the combination?"

The banker nodded grimly. "Mr. Potter was the only one."

Dub gazed out across the crowd until he saw the town blacksmith. "Wilbur, can you get that vault opened?"

"I can but it'll take a while and I'll ruin the vault's door."

"Do it anyway," Dub ordered. "As fast as you can!"

Wilbur raced down the street toward his shop. Longarm spent a few minutes listening to the crowd and then he started for the stable. Dub overtook him. "Where are you going?"

"After Pete and the town's money."

"How do you know—"

"I just do," Longarm interrupted. "Who else would have done it? And that bloody boot print was fresh. What you almost certainly have in that vault, Dub, is a dead banker and some empty shelves where cash used to be stored. There's no time to wait for the vault to be broken into."

Sheriff Turner touched his sleeve. "When I went out to the ranch, I woke Maria and spoke to her. I told her that something might have happened to her father and—"

"Her what?" Longarm cried.

"Mr. Potter was her *father*. She was his illegitimate child. He loved Maria and so do I. We have plans to get married. Mr. Potter approved. I was going to live at the ranch and run it when he was in town."

Longarm stared at the young sheriff and tried to make sense of it all. "What about the story of her father, José, and her mother and—"

"All lies," Dub confessed. "All lies to cover up Maria's illegitimacy. But Mr. Potter told me because he could see we'd fallen in love. I gave him my word never to tell her story. He changed his will and I'm in it along with Maria."

"So if he's dead, you'll both inherit *everything*?"

"Maria will, and as her new husband, so will I. It's a little more complicated than that . . . I'll get a large sum of money every five years, and our children will get their share as well. Mr. Potter was very careful about things, and he made it all clear in his will. He was a hard man . . . but a decent enough one."

"And what about the story that Maria has . . . has some serious physical problems?"

"That was true a few years ago, but she's fine now."

Longarm knew there was probably a lot more to this story, but he would not let it slow him down in his pursuit of Pete Rafter . . . the killer. He didn't know what had happened to Willie Benton, but maybe when he caught Pete, that part of the story would also be revealed.

"I'm leaving as soon as I can saddle a horse and grab a few things."

"I'm going with you," Dub insisted.

"I don't need your help."

"Yes you do," Dub insisted. "Because your eyes are

telling me that you mean to kill Pete Rafter and not arrest him. I can't let you do that, Custis. I'm still carrying a badge even if you aren't."

"Then let's stop jawing and get to hunting," Longarm said tightly.

Chapter 24

Pete's horse went lame just after crossing the border into Utah and seeing the Green River. He led the animal for two miles, and when the horse grew increasingly reluctant to move, Pete considered shooting it but relented. He unsaddled and bridled the animal and set it free. "If I am being followed, it would help if you kept walking but I don't suppose you will."

Pete set out on foot. He made it eight miles chewing on bread and jerky and sipping Mr. Potter's whiskey until he became too drunk to walk any farther. He was tired and yet so happy he couldn't stop smiling. He had nineteen thousand dollars in the pair of money sacks. Enough to buy him the kind of life he'd always dreamed about.

I'll go to San Francisco, he thought. *I always heard that the women there are beautiful and a man with money can take his pick.*

Pete built a campfire, a roaring big one, and he drank some more. The sparks from his fire lifted up into a night sky brilliant with stars. He fell asleep dreaming of expensive whores, cigars, and liquor. Of a closet of tailored silk suits, a gold watch, and a Chinese servant bringing him Oriental delights whenever he clapped his hands. And he wondered what it would be like to couple with an Oriental woman, and he thought it would feel very, very good. He had heard stories about how they would do things to a man that were almost unbelievable in their pleasure and creativity . . . just thinking about this gave him an erection and he carried it to sleep with him that night.

He wasn't smiling much the following morning. His head was ringing like a Chinese gong and thumping like a Comanche drum. His mouth tasted awful and his vision was cloudy. And then he remembered he didn't even have a horse to ride.

Grumbling, Pete stuffed his money sacks into his now empty saddlebags and slowly headed south. After killing Willie and having to walk so far, he had vowed never to walk more than one hundred steps at a time ever again. But here he was, walking way out in the wilderness, food gone, most of the whiskey gone, a sour stomach, and he had the scoots to boot and the accompanying stinging red ass.

Gotta get a hold of myself. I'm a rich man now. Gotta remember that life is gonna be good. Just gotta find someplace to rest up and hide. Steal . . . no, now I can buy another horse. Any horse I want.

By nightfall, Pete was staggering and back into the second bottle of whiskey. He found a place to camp, built a big fire, and since his food was gone from his saddlebags, replaced by the money, he tried to count it all over again but he kept coming up with different sums.

Gotta get some sleep. Drink some water. Need more

wood for the fire. Might be grizzly bears or cougars all around. Gotta collect some firewood.

Longarm and Dub found Pete the following afternoon at the bottom of a thirty-foot cliff. A few sticks of firewood were still in his arms. His face had taken the main brunt of the fall, and it looked like a cherry pie that a famished animal had gotten into. A shattered bottle of expensive whiskey wetly filled his right coat pocket.

Longarm climbed down from his horse and searched the body. "Nothing much on him."

"It's got to be somewhere around here," Dub said, not needing to elaborate. "He was probably collecting firewood and walked right over the cliff last night."

"Most likely he'd been drinking hard. He died on impact."

"So where is it?"

"We'll find it."

And they did. Not fifty yards from where the cliff dropped off, they found the saddlebags and what little Pete had left behind. A blanket, a new knife, and a rifle.

"Let's count the bank's money," Dub said.

"Why?" Longarm asked. "Pete couldn't have spent even a dollar since leaving Rock Springs."

"You're right about that. Should we take his body back with us?"

"If you want to hang him over the top of your horse and walk all the way back to Rock Springs, then be my guest," Longarm said. "I won't touch the bastard."

"So you think we should just leave him?"

In reply, Longarm threw the saddlebags over his shoulder and mounted his horse. "Do what you want with the body, Dub. I'm heading back to Rock Springs. There are a lot of anxious people waiting for their savings."

"Mr. Potter's burial will be soon. He was important, but not many will attend. He wasn't well liked."

"So I heard," Longarm answered. "Now that he and Lucy are both gone, I assume Amy will get the entire inheritance from her Uncle Jim—more than enough money to invest in her hat factory." He watched Dub Turner mount his horse. "Are you going to turn in your badge when we get back to town?"

Dub thought about it for a few minutes and then he nodded his head. "I'm going to marry Maria and live out at the ranch. This . . . this business has sort of taken the lawman right out of me."

"Probably a good decision," Longarm said, reining his horse back north.

"What about you?" Dub asked, trotting his horse up to join him. "Are you finished? Maybe want to marry that beautiful woman you brought to Rock Springs and go back with her to Arkansas?"

"Naw," Longarm said, pulling the brim of his hat down tighter and then nudging his horse to walk a little faster. "I'm staying single and heading back to Denver on the first train through town."

"So nothing changes for you?"

Longarm glanced sideways at Dub. He thought about the whore, Lucy Potter, and all that had happened in just a short time. "Oh," he drawled, "I think a lot has changed . . . but all on the inside."

Soon to be the ex-sheriff of Rock Springs, Dub Turner gazed at him for a few minutes as they rode up through the pines and then he said more to himself than to Longarm, "Yeah, I know exactly what you mean."

Watch for

LONGARM AND THE MISSING HUSBAND

the 435th novel in the exciting LONGARM
series from Jove

Coming in February!

GIANT-SIZED ADVENTURE FROM
AVENGING ANGEL LONGARM.

BY TABOR EVANS

2006 Giant Edition:

LONGARM AND THE
OUTLAW EMPRESS

2007 Giant Edition:

LONGARM AND
THE GOLDEN EAGLE
SHOOT-OUT

2008 Giant Edition:

LONGARM AND THE
VALLEY OF SKULLS

2009 Giant Edition:

LONGARM AND THE
LONE STAR TRACKDOWN

2010 Giant Edition:

LONGARM AND THE
RAILROAD WAR

2013 Giant Edition:

LONGARM AND
THE AMBUSH AT HOLY
DEFIANCE

penguin.com/actionwesterns

M456AS0812

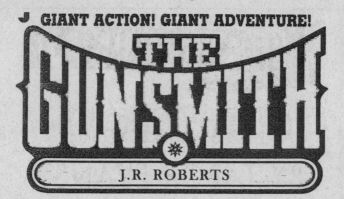

GIANT ACTION! GIANT ADVENTURE!

THE GUNSMITH

J.R. ROBERTS

penguin.com/actionwesterns

M455AS0812

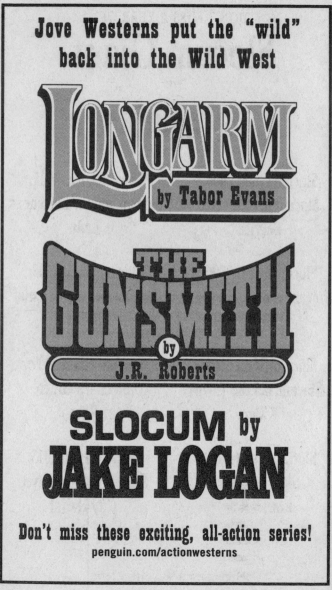